WINGBEARER

MARJORIE LIU

ILLUSTRATED BY
TENY ISSAKHANIAN

Quill Tree Books
Imprints of HarperCollinsPublishers

Quill Tree Books is an imprint of HarperCollins Publishers.
HarperAlley is an imprint of HarperCollins Publishers.

Wingbearer
 For information address HarperCollins Children's Books, a division of HarperCollins Publishers, 195 Broadway, New York, NY 10007.
www.harperalley.com
Library of Congress Control Number: 2021942269

ISBN 978-0-06-274116-5 — ISBN 978-0-06-274115-8 (pbk.)

The artist used Adobe Photoshop to create the illustrations for this book.
Typography by Catherine San Juan
21 22 23 24 25 RTLO 10 9 8 7 6 5 4 3 2 1
First Edition

Maya . . . this is for you, with all my love.
May you always soar. **—M.L.**

To my beloved grandmother, an Armenian poet
and the most beautiful of souls, Arpenik Aghakhanian
Chamras. Your legacy of love and your empowerment
of our Armenian people gave so many the wings they
needed to soar. I love you for all eternity, my
sireli medzmama jan. **—T.I.**

I DON'T KNOW HOW IT BEGAN.
THAT'S THE TRUTH, I PROMISE.

THE WINGS TELL ME THAT BIRDS HAVE ALWAYS BEEN IMMORTAL. THAT THEIR SPIRITS LIVE FOREVER, RETURNING TO THIS TREE TO BE REBORN. AND I ASK THEM, "WELL, WHAT ABOUT THE REST OF US?"

THEY HAVE NO ANSWER.

BUT I THINK THAT IF BIRDS HAVE A TREE, THEN SO MUST EVERY OTHER CREATURE. AND WHEN WE DIE, OUR SOULS TRAVEL TO THAT PLACE WHERE WE REST, JUST LIKE BIRDS, UNTIL WE ARE REBORN.

UNLESS, OF COURSE, SOMEONE -- OR SOMETHING -- GETS IN THE WAY.

I DON'T KNOW HOW IT BEGAN FOR ME, EITHER.

JUST ONE MORE STEP, ZULI... YOU'RE ALMOST WALKING...

THERE'S A LOT I DON'T KNOW, BUT I'M TRYING TO CHANGE THAT. ADVENTURES HELP. ADVENTURES ARE GOOD FOR MAKING OUR WORLDS BIGGER...

...AND OUR HEARTS, TOO.

HEARTS GROW. I THINK A HEART COULD GROW AS BIG AS THE TREE, IF THERE WAS ENOUGH SPACE AROUND IT.

AND THAT WOULD BE AN AWFULLY BIG HEART.

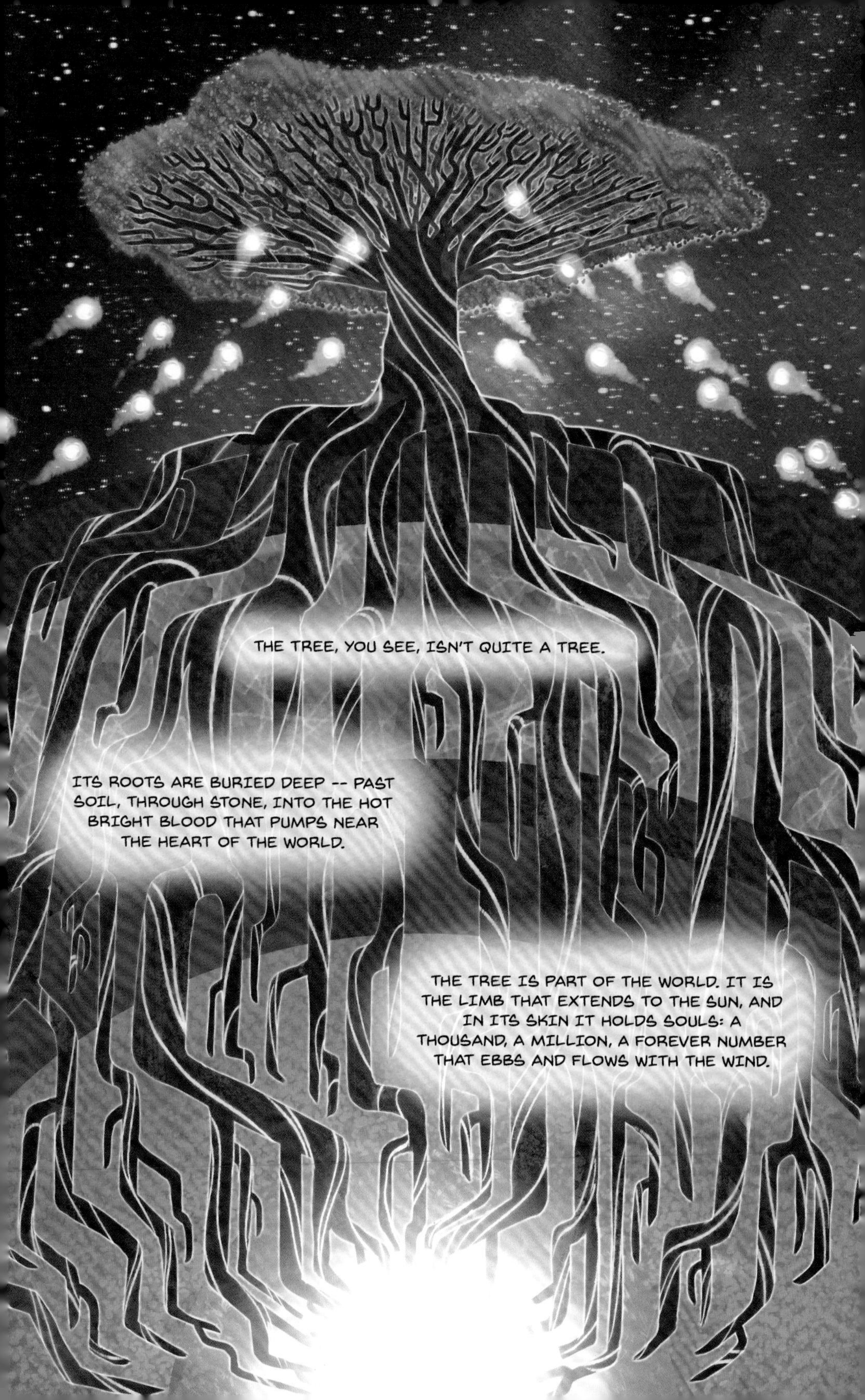

THE TREE, YOU SEE, ISN'T QUITE A TREE.

ITS ROOTS ARE BURIED DEEP -- PAST SOIL, THROUGH STONE, INTO THE HOT BRIGHT BLOOD THAT PUMPS NEAR THE HEART OF THE WORLD.

THE TREE IS PART OF THE WORLD. IT IS THE LIMB THAT EXTENDS TO THE SUN, AND IN ITS SKIN IT HOLDS SOULS: A THOUSAND, A MILLION, A FOREVER NUMBER THAT EBBS AND FLOWS WITH THE WIND.

THE TREE HOLDS THE SOULS OF DEAD BIRDS.
AND THE TREE HOLDS ME.
BUT I'M NOT DEAD.
NOT YET.

LOOK, FROWLY! WE HAVE A NEW ARRIVAL!
SOFTLY, CHILD, SOFTLY.
IT'S OKAY, LITTLE ONE. YOU'RE SAFE.
DON'T BE FRIGHTENED.
YOU'VE RETURNED TO THE TREE, THAT'S ALL.

YOU'LL HAVE YOUR WINGS AGAIN SOON.
DREAM OF THE WIND CARRYING YOU INTO THE SKY. ANY PAIN YOU SUFFERED, YOU'LL SOON FORGET.
WHAT'S THAT?
NO, I'VE NEVER SEEN A RIVER.
LIKE A RAIN SHOWER, EXCEPT ON THE GROUND?
YOU'LL HAVE TO TELL ME MORE WHEN YOU RETURN. YOU'LL BE FLYING AWAY IN JUST A DAY OR TWO, I THINK...
...BACK INTO THE WORLD.
ZULI! HURRY!
IT'S ALREADY TIME?
BUT THAT WAS SO FAST!
BACK TO THE SKY WITH YOU...
...ABOUT TO BE BORN AGAIN.
YOU MUST MISS YOUR WINGS.

HAVE A BEAUTIFUL LIFE! MAYBE YOU'LL BE BORN NEAR THE SEA THIS TIME...
I WISH I COULD SEE THE SEA.
CRICK!
!!!
FAREWELL!
SAFE TRAVELS!
UNTIL WE MEET AGAIN! I CAN'T WAIT TO HEAR YOUR STORIES!
WE ALWAYS MEET AGAIN.

THAT'S THE BEAUTY OF THE TREE.
IT'S HOME, FOREVER. FOR ME.
"T'AIA... I KNOW I PROMISED NOT TO ASK ANYMORE..."
I JUST NEVER REALIZED HOW FRAGILE HOME COULD BE.
NO, ZULI. THERE HAVE BEEN NO SONGS FROM THE BIRDS. NO STORIES.
NOT A ONE.
WE DO NOT YET KNOW WHERE YOU COME FROM.
OR WHAT YOU ARE.

ONE DAY THERE'LL BE A WHISPER.
THERE CAN'T BE JUST ONE OF ME. RIGHT, FROWLY?
IT'S NOT LIKELY. BUT ONE SHOULD NOT RUSH TO ASSUME.
THERE'S NOT JUST ONE OF ANYTHING. I KNOW THAT MUCH. WHERE I'M FROM MUST BE...VERY FAR AWAY, THAT'S ALL.
FAR FROM BIRDSONG.
NOTHING IS FAR FROM BIRDSONG, LITTLE ONE.
ESPECIALLY YOU.

YOU SHOULD NOT KEEP LYING TO THE CHILD. IT WILL COME TO NO GOOD, IN THE END.
WHAT SHE IS CANNOT BE DENIED. SHE WILL GROW. SHE WILL AGE. IT IS NOT FAIR THAT SHE BE ALONE.
SHE CANNOT STAY HERE FOREVER, NO MATTER HOW MUCH WE LOVE HER.
HUSH.
HUSH AND LISTEN.
DO YOU HEAR IT?
THE SILENCE.
THERE ARE NO SOULS IN THE WIND.

YOU'D THINK THAT LIVING IN THE TREE WOULD BE BORING, BUT NO SINGLE DAY IS EVER THE SAME.

EVERYTHING IS ALWAYS CHANGING.

EACH DAY IS NEW.
AND THERE'S ALWAYS A SURPRISE.
THE WINGS TELL ME THAT I WAS THE GREATEST SURPRISE OF ALL.
WHO DO YOU THINK IS GOING TO JOIN US TODAY?
AND THEY BELIEVE THAT WHAT HAPPENS ONCE WILL ALWAYS HAPPEN TWICE.
I HOPE THAT'S TRUE.

IT MUST BE TRUE.
IF THERE'S ONE OF ME, THERE MUST BE TWO.
HERE WE ARE!
RIGHT WHERE THE WINGS FOUND ME.
HELLO?
IS ANYONE THERE?
OH.
WELL, THERE'S ALWAYS TOMORROW.

WHAT...IS THAT?
IN ALL MY YEARS I'VE NEVER SEEN ANYTHING LIKE IT.
IT LOOKS...DEAD.
WAIT, LITTLE RED! SLOW DOWN! WHAT'S HAPPENED?
OH NO!
THIS CANNOT BE!

WHAT'S WRONG?
COME! COME SEE!
I JUST SAW ANOTHER ONE OF THOSE. WHAT IS IT?
A LEAF WITHOUT A SOUL.
BUT THAT'S... IMPOSSIBLE.
T'AIA! T'AIA!
WHAT HAS HAPPENED?
WE DO NOT YET KNOW.

MY FELLOW GUARDIANS...THE SOULS OF BIRDS HAVE GONE SILENT. WE CANNOT HEAR THEM BEYOND THE TREE.
AND THE NEW BUDS THAT APPEAR UPON THE BRANCHES ARE SHRIVELED AND DEAD.
BUT THIS TREE IS WHERE BIRDS REST WHEN THEY DIE.
WHERE COULD THEIR SOULS HAVE GONE?
ZULI!
THERE HAS TO BE ONE NEW SOUL. AT LEAST ONE.
IT CAN'T BE TRUE.
ZULI, PLEASE.
THE WIND IS SILENT. THERE ARE NO NEW VOICES.

MAYBE...MAYBE BIRDS AREN'T DYING? JUST FOR A NIGHT...?
NO, LITTLE ONE. FROM WHAT THE TREE TELLS US, THE WORLD OUTSIDE IS UNCHANGED.
BIRDS STILL LIVE AND DIE.
T'AIA, I'M GETTING REALLY SCARED.
I SUPPOSE YOU ARE RIGHT TO BE.
IF DEATH HAS NOT BEEN STOPPED...
...THEN SOMETHING IS HAPPENING TO THE SOULS OF THE BIRDS.

EVERY END IS A BEGINNING.
THAT'S WHAT THE WINGS SAY.

BUT I NEVER FELT THE TRUTH OF IT UNTIL THIS MOMENT.

ALL I'VE KNOWN IS THE TREE, AND THE WINGS, AND THE BIRDS.

THE WORLD BEYOND NEVER INTRUDED.

EVEN THOUGH I WANTED IT TO.

NOW IT HAS, AND ALL I WANT TO DO IS HIDE.

UNLESS WE FIND THOSE MISSING SOULS AND DISCOVER WHAT HAS PREVENTED THEM FROM REACHING THE TREE, IT WILL BE THE END OF ALL BIRDS.

THE LAST LEAF THAT BREAKS FROM THE TREE WILL BE THE LAST BIRD BORN.

NO CREATURE CAN LIVE WITHOUT ITS SOUL, ZULI.

NOT YOU. NOT I.

LIVE LONG. FLY SAFE.
FAREWELL, LITTLE ONE.
SOMEONE HAS TO GO FIND THOSE MISSING SOULS...
...AND STOP WHATEVER'S DONE THIS.
I COULD GO, THOUGH I'VE NEVER BEEN IN THE WORLD --
NO.
INDEED, YOU CAN'T LEAVE THE TREE.
BUT, T'AIA --
YOU WILL STAY HERE.
I NEED YOU ALL TO DO SOMETHING FOR ME.
AFTER ALL, FOUR HEADS ARE BETTER THAN JUST ONE, RIGHT?
EXCEPT WHEN THEY'RE NOT.

WE ALL KNOW HOW MUCH BIRDS LOVE TO TALK.
FIND THE YOUNGEST LEAVES, THE ONES THAT BUDDED JUST BEFORE THIS STARTED.
ASK THEM IF THEY SAW ANYTHING...DIFFERENT.
ASK A BIRD FOR A STORY AND SHE'LL TELL YOU TWO.
GREETINGS! I'M VERY SORRY TO BOTHER YOU, BUT I WONDERED IF I COULD ASK SOME QUESTIONS?
THAT'S VERY INTERESTING.
TELL THE OTHER GUARDIANS TO START TALKING TO THE SOULS AS WELL.
THE OTHER THING ABOUT BIRDS IS THAT THEY'RE CURIOUS. THEY NOTICE EVERYTHING.
I KNEW IT, LITTLE RED! WHAT'D THEY SAY?
MAYBE ONE OF THEM NOTICED SOMETHING USEFUL WHILE ALIVE THAT MIGHT EXPLAIN WHAT HAPPENED TO THE SOULS OF THE BIRDS.

T'AIA, ONE OF THE SOULS TOLD LITTLE RED THEY SAW SOMETHING STRANGE JUST BEFORE THEIR DEATH.
INSIDE A HOLLOW TREE MADE OF STONE.
AND THERE WAS BLUE LIGHT? LIKE FIRE?
DO YOU KNOW WHAT IT MEANS?
IT MEANS WE SHOULD NOT BE HASTY.
FROWLY IS RIGHT...BUT ANOTHER DAY HAS PASSED AND NOT A SINGLE SOUL HAS COME TO US.
SOMETHING *MUST* BE DONE.
SOMEONE *MUST* BE SENT.
PERFECT. I'LL START PACKING MY THINGS --
LITTLE RED WILL GO.
HE IS THE OLDEST AND FASTEST OF OUR CORPOREAL HELPERS.

LITTLE RED SHOULDN'T GO ALONE. I'LL GO, TOO.
PERHAPS WE SHOULD SLEEP ON IT --
ZULI...A LITTLE BIRD WITH WINGS CAN TRAVEL FARTHER AND FASTER THAN A LITTLE GIRL ON TWO FEET.
THERE IS NO SHAME IN THAT.
BUT I WANT TO HELP... EVEN THOUGH I'M SCARED.
YOU ALREADY HAVE HELPED. IT WAS YOUR IDEA TO QUESTION THE SOULS. LET US SEE NOW WHAT COMES OF IT.
FLY SWIFTLY, LITTLE RED. TAKE NO CHANCES.
RETURN TO US WITHIN SEVEN SUNRISES, NO MATTER WHAT YOU DO -- OR DO NOT -- FIND.
THAT BIRD IS MAYBE A LITTLE TOO FAST, IF YOU ASK ME.
BE CAREFUL, LITTLE RED.

IF A SOUL CAN'T REACH THE TREE, WHY IS THERE EVEN THE BEGINNING OF A BUD?
THE TREE SENSES THE BIRD'S DEATH, AND TRIES TO MAKE A HOME FOR THE SOUL.
SO MANY BIRDS ARE DYING.
IT'S BEEN MORE THAN SEVEN DAYS, T'AIA.

OH, LITTLE ONE.
YOU MUST LET HER GO, T'AIA.
WE CANNOT PROTECT ZULI FOREVER.
NOR CAN WE VENTURE FROM THE TREE -- AND THOSE MISSING SOULS *MUST* BE FOUND. SHE MAY BE ABLE TO DO IT. SHE HAS THE GIFT.
SHE KNOWS NOTHING OF WHAT EXISTS BEYOND THESE BRANCHES. WHAT CAN SHE DO IN THE WORLD, ALONE?
WHAT SHE ESCAPED WAS SO TERRIBLE...
THOSE DAYS ARE LONG OVER. TIME PASSES DIFFERENTLY IN THE WORLD BEYOND.
AND WHAT CAN SHE DO HERE?
NOTHING, T'AIA.
LET HER GO. LET HER LIVE. SO SHE CAN BECOME SOMETHING. AND IN THAT BECOMING, PERHAPS SAVE US ALL.

RUNNING OFF?
I HAVE TO. LITTLE RED HAS BEEN GONE TOO LONG. HE MIGHT NEED HELP.
AH, ZULI.
YOU WERE SO SMALL.
A NESTLING. BROUGHT TO THE TREE, BUT IN THE FLESH.

WE MADE YOU OURS.
CARED FOR YOU.
LOVED YOU.
I'M SO GRATEFUL FOR YOUR LOVE... AND I LOVE YOU, TOO. THAT'S WHY I'M LEAVING. I HAVE TO AT LEAST *TRY* TO HELP.
I KNOW, ZULI. YOU ARE AS MUCH A GUARDIAN AS THE REST OF US.
DON'T DO THIS... THE WORLD IS TERRIBLY UNSAFE.
YOU'VE NEVER SAID THAT BEFORE, FROWLY.
AND YET, IT'S TRUE. WHICH IS WHY ONE OF YOU MUST ACCOMPANY HER.
YOUR CORPOREAL MEMORIES WILL HAVE FADED, BUT YOU'LL HAVE SOME SENSE OF HOW TO GUIDE ZULI.

YOU CAN'T SEND CHEERA. SHE'S NOT A STRONG FLIER.
THAT IS WHY I'M SENDING YOU, FROWLY.
YOU ARE THE MIGHTIEST OF THE CORPOREALS.
YOU WILL KNOW HOW TO GUIDE ZULI... EVEN IF YOU DON'T REMEMBER HOW, AT THIS EXACT MOMENT.
I'M SO GLAD YOU'RE COMING, FROWLY!
WAIT --
I FIND IT DIFFICULT TO SAY GOODBYE.
SO LET'S NOT SAY GOODBYE. LET'S PERHAPS THINK THIS THROUGH.
TAKE CARE OF HER, FROWLY. BE WISE AND BE BRAVE. AND FAREWELL, ZULI, FAREWELL.
IT'S NOT FOREVER, T'AIA. I'LL COME BACK.
WE MAY NOT MEET AGAIN.

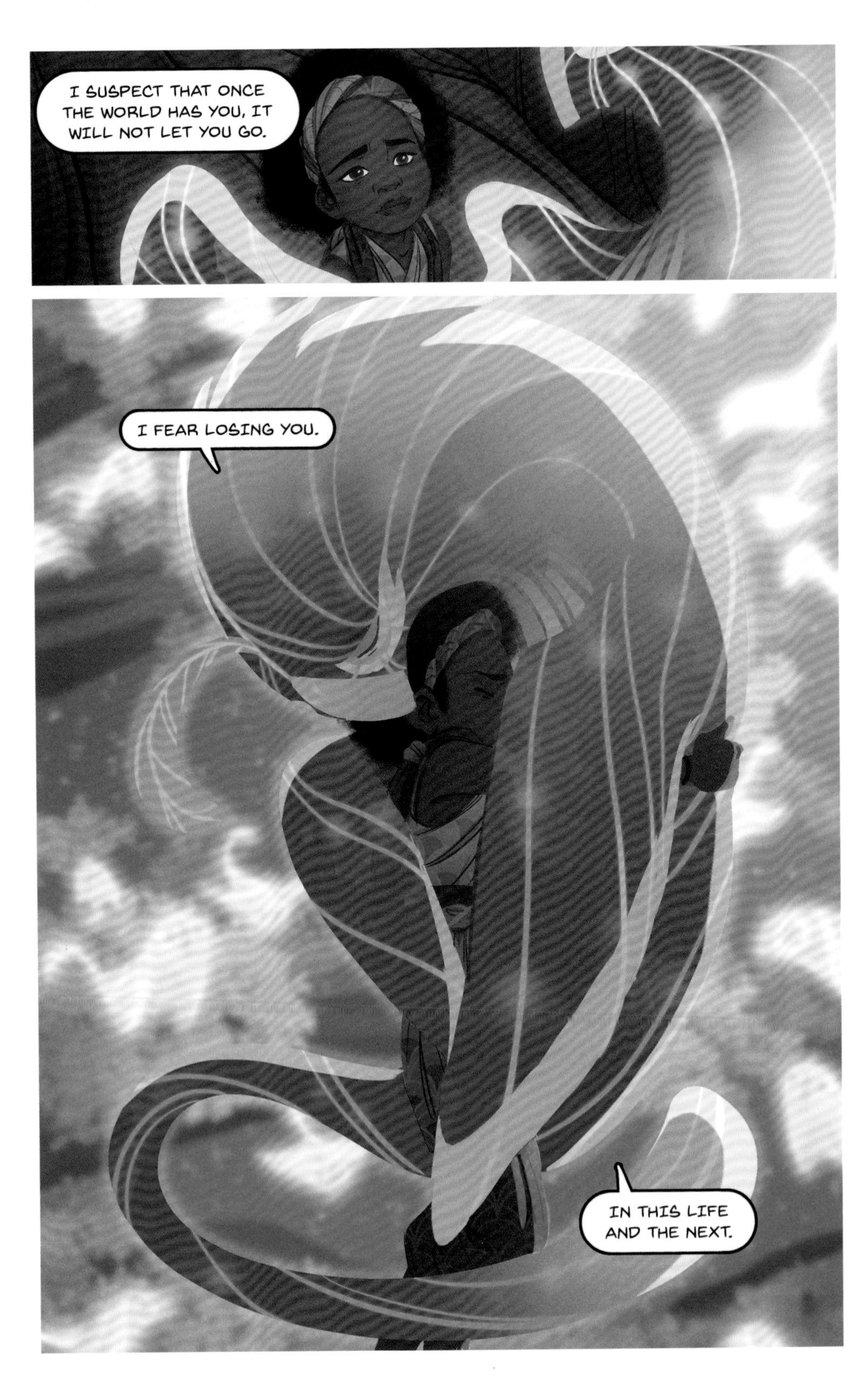
I SUSPECT THAT ONCE THE WORLD HAS YOU, IT WILL NOT LET YOU GO.
I FEAR LOSING YOU.
IN THIS LIFE AND THE NEXT.

"WE GUARDIANS ARE PART OF THE TREE, ZULI. AS MUCH AS ITS BRANCHES AND ROOTS."

"AND EVERY TREE, NO MATTER HOW FAR AWAY OR STRANGE, IS PART OF THIS TREE."

"REMEMBER THAT. REMEMBER THE LOVE OF TREES, WHICH IS OUR LOVE. IT MIGHT HELP YOU, ONE DAY."

I'VE NEVER BEEN SO FAR FROM THE TREE...THIS DEEP INTO THE ARBOR LANDS.
FROWLY, IT'S SO QUIET HERE.
I SHOULD HOPE IT'S QUIET. THIS IS WHERE TREES COME WHEN THEY DREAM.
IS THIS THE BARRIER? THE LIVING WORLD IS ON THE OTHER SIDE?
SADLY, YES.
THIS IS A VERY BAD IDEA, IF YOU ASK ME.
ALL THIS TIME, I'VE WAITED FOR MY FAMILY TO FIND ME... BUT I GUESS I WAS NEVER BRAVE ENOUGH TO GO LOOKING.

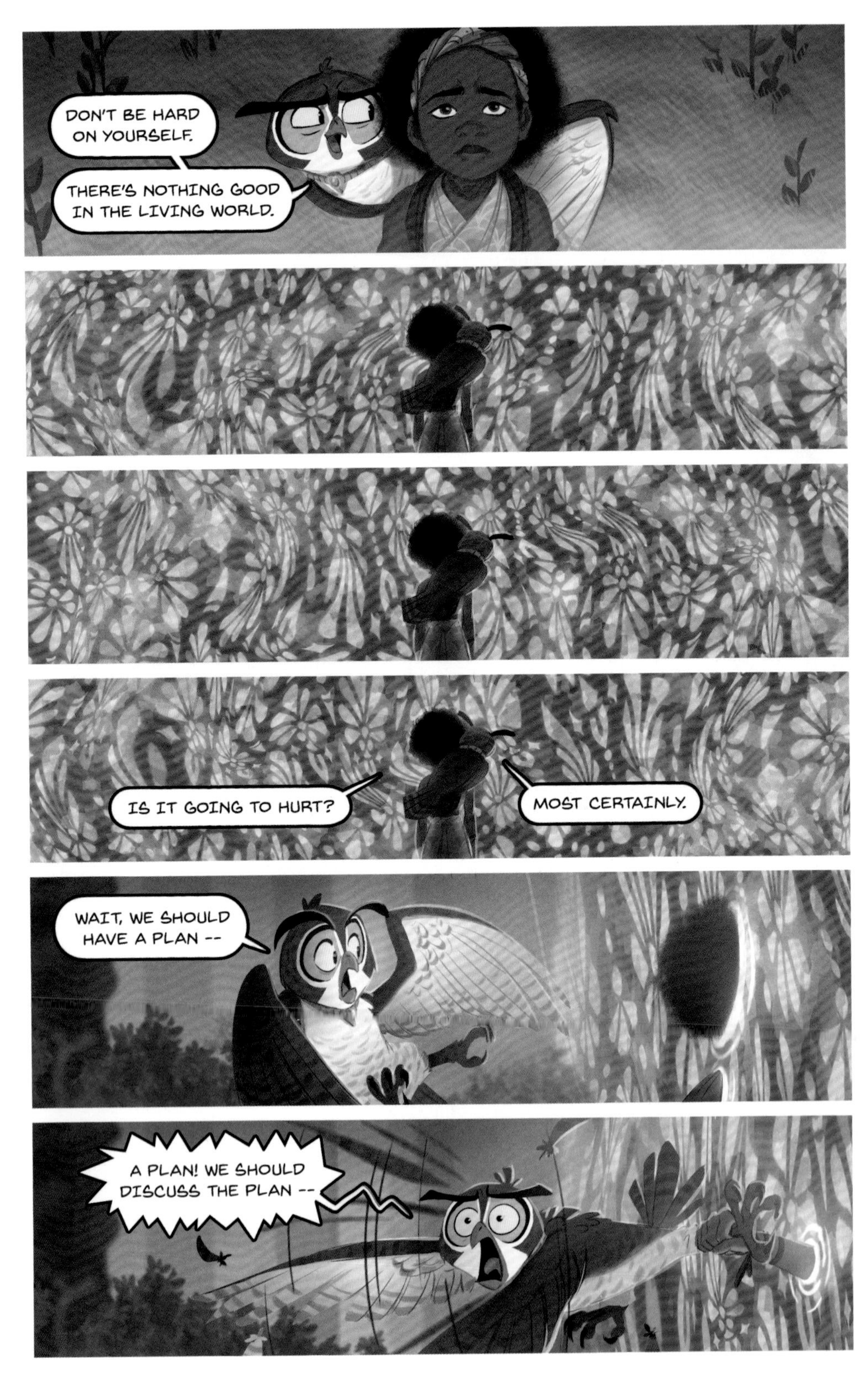
DON'T BE HARD ON YOURSELF.
THERE'S NOTHING GOOD IN THE LIVING WORLD.
IS IT GOING TO HURT?
MOST CERTAINLY.
WAIT, WE SHOULD HAVE A PLAN --
A PLAN! WE SHOULD DISCUSS THE PLAN --

VSHOOOM!
FROWLY...
IS THIS THE WORLD?

BUT WHERE ARE THE TREES?
NOTHING IS ALIVE.
IT'S SO...COLD.
AND SAD.
SOMETHING IS WRONG...
THIS DOESN'T *FEEL* RIGHT.
FROWLY, WAIT --

OH NO.
I DIDN'T KNOW THAT WORLDS COULD DIE, TOO.
HOW MUCH TIME HAS PASSED, I WONDER?
FROWLY?
WHAT DO YOU MEAN?

THE GUARDIANS ONCE TOLD ME THAT TIME MOVES DIFFERENTLY BETWEEN THE TREE AND THE WORLD BEYOND...BUT THIS...IS MORE THAN I EXPECTED.
YOU KNOW WHERE WE ARE?
I SHOULD. I DO. I THINK I MUST.
WHAT A STRANGE FEELING, ZULI. I DIDN'T REMEMBER THIS PLACE UNTIL I SAW IT...BUT I KNOW I WAS HERE. I KNOW IT. I CAN SEE IT IN MY HEAD, AS IT ONCE WAS.
BUT I DON'T REMEMBER ITS NAME, OR WHY I LEFT.
FROWLY, I'M BEGINNING TO REALIZE I MADE A MISTAKE.
OH, THANK GOODNESS --
I ALWAYS ASSUMED YOU WERE JUST A DIFFERENT KIND OF GUARDIAN... BUT YOU'RE NOT, ARE YOU?
I SUPPOSE THAT'S TRUE.
YOU'RE FROM THE WORLD, JUST LIKE ME.

MY FAMILY MUST HAVE BEEN HERE, TOO, BEFORE THEY LEFT ME AT THE TREE. MAYBE THIS IS WHERE I'M FROM!
WELL, LOOK AT THAT.
AFTER ALL THESE YEARS OF WAITING FOR THE GATE TO OPEN.
PERHAPS THE PLAN ISN'T SO FOOLHARDY, AFTER ALL.
WAKE, YOU FOOLS!
THE CHILD HAS RETURNED!

IT WILL BE BEST IF WE KEEP GOING UNTIL WE'RE CLEAR OF THE CITY.
I KNOW...
BUT THERE'S SO MUCH TO SEE.
WHO IS THAT?
I...COULDN'T POSSIBLY KNOW.

THERE'S NOTHING OF INTEREST HERE. NOTHING AT ALL. WE SHOULD JUST KEEP FLYING. AND FAST.
I DO NOT LIKE THE FEEL OF THIS PLACE.
DO OUR FACES LOOK ALIKE?
I SUPPOSE, BUT ONE SHOULD NOT JUMP TO CONCLUSIONS.
I CAN'T HELP IT. I'VE NEVER SEEN ANYTHING THAT MIGHT LOOK LIKE ME.

HELLO THERE!
IT'S GOOD TO SEE FRIENDLY FEATHERS! WON'T YOU COME DOWN FOR A MOMENT AND CHAT WITH US? WE'RE IN NEED OF DIRECTIONS!
ZULI...THOSE ARE VULTURES...
...AND THEY ARE NOT KNOWN FOR SMALL TALK...
OWL IS RIGHT.
WE WATCH. NOT MUCH TALK.
OH, BUT WE NEED HELP. WE'RE TRYING TO FIND --
SHE LOOK SICK TO YOU?
NOT YET. WILL BE SOON IF SHE STAY HERE.

EXCUSE --
MIGHT BE DYING.
HARD TO TELL.
WAIT --
THEN AGAIN, EVERYONE DYING.
IN CASE YOU DIE, WE FOLLOW.
MAYBE YOU DIE TONIGHT.
I'M NOT DYING. I HAVE IMPORTANT THINGS TO DO BEFORE THAT HAPPENS.
I'VE GOT TO SAVE THE SOULS OF THE BIRDS. YOUR SOULS, AS A MATTER OF FACT. OTHERWISE, WHEN YOU DIE, YOU WON'T BE REBORN.
REBORN? SOULS? HA HA HA...
BORN AGAIN IN STOMACHS!
DEAD IS DEAD. NOTHING ELSE. JUST FOOD FOR THE LIVING.

HAHA!
HAHA!
HAHA!
HAHA!
BUT THAT'S NOT TRUE!
DON'T WASTE YOUR ENERGY, ZULI.
HOW COULD THEY NOT KNOW, FROWLY?
WHY WOULD THEY? WHO REMEMBERS ANYTHING?
I, FOR ONE, STILL DON'T RECALL ANYTHING MORE ABOUT THIS CITY. EXCEPT THAT BEING HERE MAKES ME AFRAID...AND SAD.
I AM ALSO COMPLETELY CERTAIN WE SHOULD NOT SPEND THE NIGHT.
I'M NOT SURE WE'LL HAVE A CHOICE.
IT'S GETTING DARK.
MEEP!
WHAT...WHAT'S THAT SOUND...AND THAT FEELING ON MY SKIN...?
OOOO...LAAAA...OOOO...LAAAA...
GASP

LOATHSOME CHILD...
FROWLY! FLY! FLY!
I CAN'T! MY WINGS ARE FROZEN WITH FEAR!

HOW SMALL YOU ARE...
ZZZZ
LET GO!

FROWLY!
RUN, ZULI!
ZULI! RUN!
AHHH!
NO!
MONSTERS!
MONSTERS EVERYWHERE!

FROWLY -- THERE'S A STRANGE LIGHT...
WHY ARE YOU STOPPING?!
GET BACK!

GASP
ZULI!

NO!
NNGGH!
STAY BEHIND ME!
OOF!

ARE YOU HURT?

WELL, YOU'RE NOT BLEEDING. GOT ALL YOUR LIMBS.
SIGH
THIS IS THE WORST LUCK. I JUST GOT HERE.
I WAS GONNA FIND GOOD SCAVENGE THIS TIME, I KNOW IT.
NOW I WON'T EVER BE ABLE TO COME BACK, NOT WITH THE CITY SO DANGEROUS.
I SHOULD PROBABLY BLAME YOU.

COME ON. I KNOW YOUR LEGS STILL WORK. WE HAVE TO GET OUT OF THE CITY.
WHAT ARE YOU DOING?
WE CAN'T STAY HERE, FROWLY.
BUT HE'S A STRANGER! JUST BECAUSE HE HELPED US DOES NOT MAKE HIM SAFE.
MAYBE NOT.
BUT HE CAN'T BE MORE DANGEROUS THAN THOSE THINGS UP THERE.
I'M NOT SURE ABOUT THAT. THERE'S SOMETHING FAMILIAR ABOUT HIM... I WISH I COULD REMEMBER WHAT IT IS...
I DO KNOW I DON'T LIKE IT.

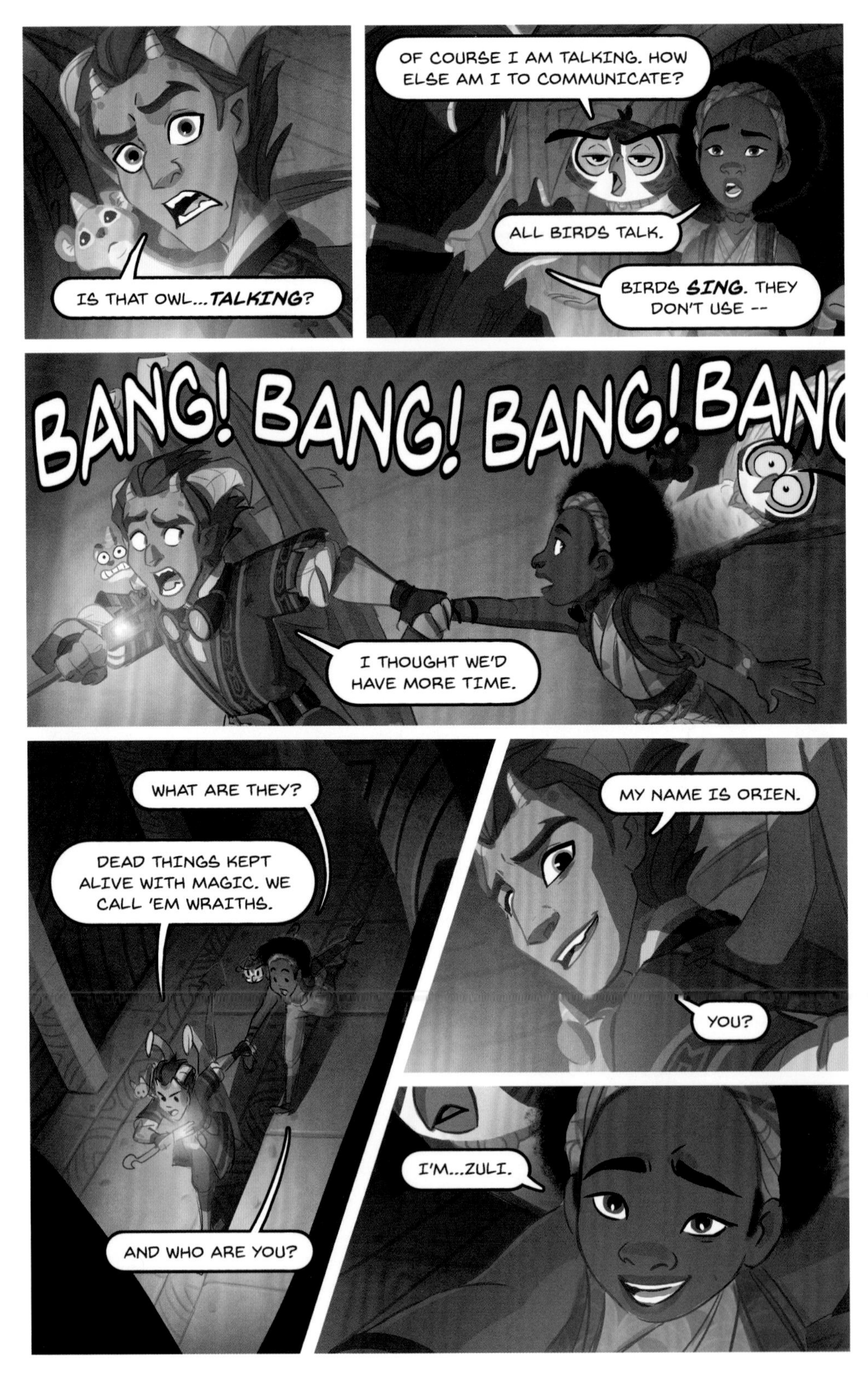
IS THAT OWL...**TALKING**?
OF COURSE I AM TALKING. HOW ELSE AM I TO COMMUNICATE?
ALL BIRDS TALK.
BIRDS **SING**. THEY DON'T USE --
BANG! BANG! BANG! BANG
I THOUGHT WE'D HAVE MORE TIME.
WHAT ARE THEY?
DEAD THINGS KEPT ALIVE WITH MAGIC. WE CALL 'EM WRAITHS.
AND WHO ARE YOU?
MY NAME IS ORIEN.
YOU?
I'M...ZULI.

THIS IS YOUR IDEA OF AN ESCAPE?
UH, NOT REALLY. I THINK I TOOK A WRONG TURN.
IT'S TOO LATE TO GO BACK.
SO WE'LL CLIMB DOWN.
CLIMB?!
WE DON'T NEED TO CLIMB.

I KNOW WHAT YOU ARE...
AHHH! YOU HAVE WINGS!
THAT'S AMAZING!
HANG ON!
OH DEAR.
OH DEAR.
YOUR WINGS AREN'T LARGE ENOUGH, BOY! NOT TO SUPPORT YOU BOTH!

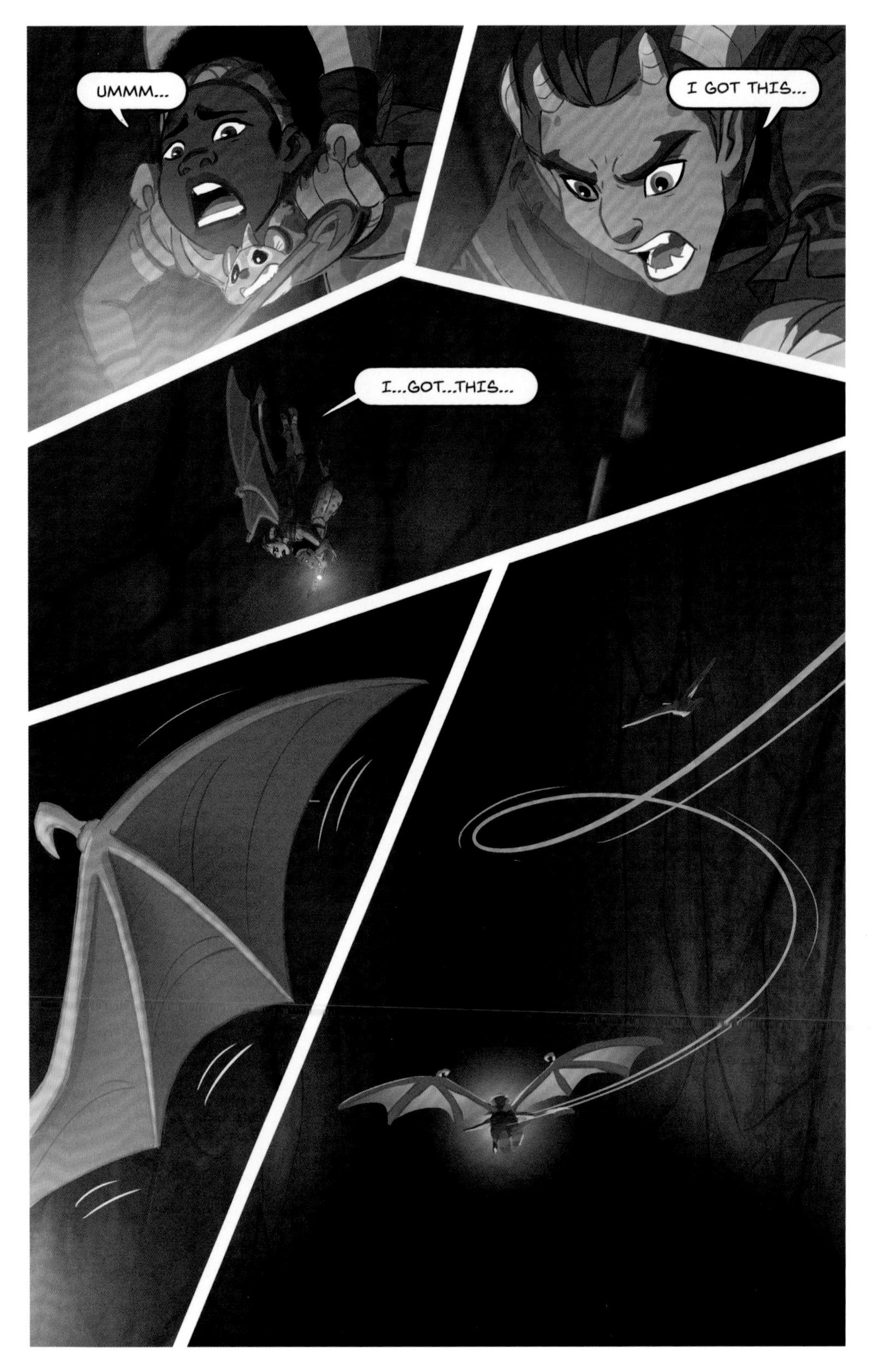
UMMM...
I GOT THIS...
I...GOT...THIS...

WOOO!
I'M FLYING!!!

THIS IS INCREDIBLE!

YOU'RE STILL GOING TOO FAST --

KSHHT

I'VE NEVER FLOWN BEFORE. THAT WAS...WONDERFUL!
GOOD. I THINK I'M GONNA PUKE.
ARE THESE MORE STATUES?
HUH? NO, THESE ARE *BONES.*
OF DEAD DRAGONS.

SO THIS IS WHAT THE DEAD LOOK LIKE.
DO WE HAVE BONES, TOO, FROWLY?
I'D RATHER NOT THINK ABOUT IT.
WAIT UP! I HAVE SO MANY QUESTIONS!
SO DO I.
I SAW YOU HURT THE WRAITHS WITH THAT THING.
ONLY MAGIC CAN DO THAT.
YOU HURT THEM, TOO.
I *SCARED* THEM. THEY HATE LIGHT. BUT SCARING IS *NOT* HURTING.
BUT WHAT'S MAGIC --
AH!
WHAT IS *THIS*?
A RIVER.
BUT I THOUGHT RIVERS WERE BIGGER...AND IN THE MIDDLE OF FORESTS.
WELL...RIVERS ARE EVERYWHERE. WATER GOES WHERE IT WANTS.
WATER FEELS SO GOOD!
IT'S LIKE...LIKE...THE WIND! EXCEPT HEAVIER AND TEARFUL!
YOU'VE NEVER SEEN WATER BEFORE? NOT EVEN RAIN?
WHAT HAVE YOU BEEN DRINKING YOUR WHOLE LIFE? HOW HAVE YOU BATHED?

WELL...I...I DON'T KNOW.
I DON'T REMEMBER EVER DRINKING WATER.
IT NEVER CROSSED MY MIND THAT I NEEDED TO.
THIS IS GETTING VERY STRANGE.
I MEAN, SURE, YOU'VE ONLY GOT A TALKING OWL, AND YOUR BRACELET IS OLD MAGIC, AND YOU DON'T KNOW WHAT WATER IS.

FROWLY...AM I ALIVE?
I MEAN...I WASN'T DEAD WHEN I WAS LIVING IN THE TREE, WAS I?
YOU ARE MORE ALIVE THAN MOST OF US WILL EVER HOPE TO BE.
THE TREE IS NOT THE WORLD, THAT'S ALL. THE RULES ARE DIFFERENT.
I'D FORGOTTEN HOW DIFFERENT.
YOU HAVE A LOT TO LEARN, ZULI. MORE THAN YOU REALIZE.
YOU MAY NOT LIKE IT. AND I MAY NOT LIKE REMEMBERING.
I NEVER MISSED THIRST OR HUNGER, THAT'S FOR CERTAIN.
MY STOMACH FEELS HOLLOW. MAYBE THAT'S HUNGER?
OR MAYBE IT'S THE FEAR...

FINALLY...TREES. WHERE ARE WE?
THE BASE OF THE MOUNTAIN.
THAT'S WHERE WE WERE? ALL THE WAY UP THERE?
THE SIRIC BUILT THEIR CITIES HIGH IN THE MOUNTAINS. IF YOU HAVE WINGS, YOU LIVE AS HIGH AS YOU CAN.
IS YOUR MOUNTAIN NEAR HERE?
NO. I DON'T LIVE ANYWHERE HIGH. NOT ALLOWED.
BUT YOU HAVE --
I WAS UP THERE SCAVENGING. WHAT ABOUT YOU? IS THAT WHERE YOU FOUND THE BRACELET? THAT LOOKS LIKE A SIRIC ARTIFACT.
IT'S REALLY NONE OF YOUR BUSINESS.
AND AS SOON AS WE HAVE OUR BEARINGS, WE'LL BE PARTING --
I WAS ABANDONED WHEN I WAS A BABY. THIS BRACELET WAS LEFT WITH ME. I DON'T KNOW ANYTHING ABOUT IT.

LIKE I SAID, IT'S MAGIC. IT HAS TO BE.
THERE'S NOT MUCH OF THAT ANYMORE IN THE LOWLANDS.
MAGIC? THAT'S THE THIRD TIME YOU'VE USED THAT WORD. WHAT IS IT?
MAGIC IS POWER, I GUESS. IT MEANS YOU LIVE ON A MOUNTAIN.
DEAR BOY, IT'S MORE THAN THAT.
MAGIC IS LIKE THE WIND...EXCEPT THIS WIND CAN CHANGE THE WORLD. MAGIC CAN MAKE STONES FLOAT AND METAL CATCH FIRE.
MAGIC IS AS RARE AS A PHOENIX FEATHER, BUT JUST AS DANGEROUS AND BEAUTIFUL.
SO IS IT MAGIC THAT'S STOLEN THE SOULS OF THE BIRDS, FROWLY? IS THAT WHAT WE'RE FIGHTING?
I SUSPECT SO.
SOULS OF THE BIRDS?
HAVEN'T YOU NOTICED THAT BIRDS AREN'T BEING BORN ALIVE?
THEIR SOULS ARE BEING STOLEN, WHICH MEANS THEY CAN'T BE REBORN. IF I DON'T SAVE THEM, EVERY SINGLE BIRD WILL EVENTUALLY DISAPPEAR.

NOT BEING BORN ALIVE...
I DON'T NOW ABOUT BIRDS OR SOULS, BUT I KNOW SOMEONE WHO MIGHT.
YOU DO?
WE REALLY NEED HELP. WE HAVE NO IDEA WHERE TO GO.
ZULI! A MOMENT, PLEASE...
WE SHOULDN'T TRUST HIM.
I REMEMBERED WHAT HE IS.
HE ALREADY TOLD US. HE'S ORIEN.
HE'S A GOBLIN.
THE SWORN ENEMY OF ALL GOOD WINGS. THEY'RE MONSTERS! THEY LIVE ONLY TO INVADE, AND ENSLAVE, AND...AND THEY EAT CHILDREN!

FROWLY, THAT'S NOT NICE.
HIS KIND ARE DANGEROUS!
HAVE YOU EVER SEEN A GOBLIN DO ANY OF THOSE THINGS?
NO...NOT THAT I CAN REMEMBER...
ORIEN HELPED US. AND WE NEED TO TRUST SOMEONE.
AND T'AIA ALWAYS SAID WE SHOULDN'T JUDGE SOULS.
IF THIS GOBLIN DECIDES TO EAT US THEN YOU'LL BE VERY SORRY, ZULI.

WHO IS THIS PERSON YOU THINK CAN HELP US?
THE NAINAI OF MY CLAN.
SHE KEEPS THE OLD WISDOM...
T'AIA... I HOPE YOU CAN HEAR ME.
HUH? DO YOU WORSHIP TREES?
NO. BUT THEY'RE MY FRIENDS.
WHERE ARE YOU FROM, ANYWAY?
I DON'T KNOW. I'M HOPING TO FIND OUT.
YOU DON'T...RECOGNIZE ME, DO YOU?
NO. BUT THE WORLD IS BIG, AND GOBLINS DON'T GET TO SEE MUCH OF IT.
ARE THERE OTHER KINDS OF...FEATHERLESS? MORE THAN JUST GOBLINS?

OF COURSE.
SOME HAVE WINGS, SOME DON'T...SOME WALK ON TWO LEGS, OTHERS THREE OR FOUR...SOME LIVE ON BOATS, OR IN THE MOUNTAINS, OR THE SKY...
THAT'S...WONDERFUL.
BUT THE BIRD SOULS NEVER DESCRIBED ANYTHING LIKE THAT. NEITHER DID THE GUARDIANS.
BIRDS DON'T CONCERN THEMSELVES WITH NON-BIRDS. WHAT WOULD BE THE POINT?
FROWLY.
IT'S AS IF...NO ONE WANTED ME TO KNOW ABOUT THE WORLD.
RIDICULOUS.
WHAT ARE YOU DOING?
IT'S NIGHT. YOU BOTH ARE LOUD. YOU'LL DEFINITELY ATTRACT SOMETHING ELSE THAT WANTS TO EAT US.
SO I'M GOING TO TAKE A NAP AND WE'LL START WALKING AGAIN IN A COUPLE HOURS.
YOU CAN'T! WE HAVE TO HURRY.
THEN KEEP WALKING.
MAYBE I'LL WAKE UP AND FIND OUT THIS WAS A CRAZY DREAM.

EVEN THE STARS ARE DIFFERENT HERE.
BUT THE LIGHT IS THE SAME.
SHHHHH!

I DON'T SUPPOSE THAT MAGIC BRACELET OF YOURS IS GOOD AT FINDING SCAVENGE?
ACTUALLY, NEVER MIND.
THIS PLACE HAS BEEN PICKED OVER FOR A THOUSAND YEARS. NOTHING LEFT BUT ROCK.
WAS IT A CITY LIKE THE ONE WE WERE IN?
NAH. DRAGON OUTPOST. A FEW OF THEM ALWAYS LIVED NEAR THE SIRIC.
SIGH.
I'M GONNA GET MY WINGS CLIPPED.
WHAT'S WRONG?
I WASN'T BORN INSIDE MY CLAN. THEY ADOPTED ME. BUT THERE WERE CONDITIONS.
I JUST NEED A COUPLE GOOD SCORES, AND I'LL BE SAFE.
OH.
THOSE WRAITHS, MEETING ME...
...MADE THINGS HARDER FOR YOU.
EH...IT'S OKAY. IF IT HADN'T BEEN YOU, IT WOULD HAVE BEEN SOMETHING ELSE. LIFE ISN'T EVER EASY.
CHOP!
CHOP! CREEEAK!
WELL, HERE WE ARE.
OUTSKIRTS OF CAMP.

SHHH!
THEY'RE KILLING TREES! I HAVE TO STOP THEM!
THEY'RE NOT KILLING ANYTHING!

YES, THEY ARE! TREES ARE ALIVE! THEY THINK, THEY TALK!
CUTTING THEM DOWN IS MURDER!
WOW. YOU ARE TOO MUCH.
WITHOUT WOOD, WE WOULD DIE. WE USE IT TO BUILD SHELTERS, KEEP WARM, COOK MEALS.
WE BARTER THE LOGS FOR THINGS WE NEED.
THERE'S PLENTY OF TREES. WE DON'T TAKE MORE THAN WE NEED.
IT DOESN'T MATTER. EACH ONE IS SPECIAL. AND IT'S WHERE BIRDS MAKE THEIR HOMES.
CUTTING THEM IS WRONG AND...AND DISGUSTING.
DO YOU STILL WANT TO SEE THE NAINAI?
I DON'T KNOW. IS SHE A TREE-KILLER?
YUP, DEFINITELY.
NUMBER ONE TREE-KILLER, THAT'S HER. SAME AS ME.
FINE. I SHOULDN'T HAVE BROUGHT YOU HERE ANYWAY.
NOTHING IN IT FOR ME.
JUST ANOTHER EXCUSE NOT TO LIKE A GOBLIN.
BUT YOU WON'T LIKE ANYONE IN THIS WORLD IF YOU CAN'T STAND SEEING A TREE CUT DOWN.
IGNORE HIM. GOOD RIDDANCE!

FROWLY...IS WHAT HE SAID TRUE?
WELL...YES. FEATHERLESS TWO-LEGS BUILD THEIR NESTS FROM THE BODIES OF TREES, AND BURN THEM FOR LIGHT AND HEAT...AND MAKING FOOD.
COMPLETELY BARBARIC PRACTICE.
BUT I'M A TWO-LEG. DOES THAT MEAN I'M GOING TO HAVE TO CUT DOWN TREES TO SURVIVE?
ER...
THIS WORLD IS SO HARD AND I'VE ONLY BEEN IN IT A DAY.
WAIT, WHAT ARE YOU DOING?
OH, YOU STILL WANT HELP?
...
IT'S GOING TO COST YOU.
THAT'S NOT RIGHT.
SO?
ANYWAY, I DON'T KNOW WHAT TO CHARGE YOU YET, BUT I'LL THINK OF IT LATER.

NOTHING HERE IS FREE.

HERE...
YOU SHOULD HIDE THAT BRACELET, JUST IN CASE.
IT'S ALL I HAVE OF MY FAMILY. I'VE NEVER NOT WORN IT.
THAT'S REAL NICE, BUT YOU SHOULD HIDE IT ANYWAY.
IT'LL DRAW TOO MUCH ATTENTION.
WHAT IF I LOSE IT?
THAT'S LIFE.

HEY, OWL.
THAT'S FROWLY.
TRY NOT TO TALK AROUND ANYONE ELSE, OKAY? OR...JUST MAKE OWL SOUNDS IF YOU HAVE TO. BUT NO WORDS.
AND YOU -- TRY NOT TO ACT SO WEIRD. PRETEND YOU KNOW WHAT FOOD AND DRINK ARE.
I'LL TRY.
ORIEN.
OH. HEY, KALA.
WHY, UH, ARE YOU OUT HERE, GROOMING THESE HARDHEADS?
BAD LUCK, BUT BETTER THAN YOURS, I GUESS. YOU'RE NOT CARRYING ANY OF THE SCAVENGE YOU PROMISED.
AND YOU BROUGHT STRANGERS HOME. THIS IS THE WORST TIME EVER FOR BREAKING THE RULES.
THE DRIVER WANTS HER QUOTA -- NOT SURPRISES.

ESPECIALLY STRANGE SURPRISES.
H-HOO HOOO
THEY AREN'T STAYING.
WON'T BE MORE THAN AN HOUR, I SWEAR. THE DRIVER WON'T EVEN KNOW.
YEAH, BUT YOU DON'T HAVE THE SCAVENGE...AND WHEN SHE FINDS OUT...
...YOU'RE RUNNING OUT OF CHANCES, ORIEN.
WHAT DOES SHE MEAN BY THAT?
ORIEN?
HUH?

I'VE NEVER SEEN SO MANY FEATHERLESS TWO-LEGS BEFORE.
THIS IS A SMALL CLAN. ALSO, START CALLING PEOPLE BY THEIR NAMES.
REMEMBER, WE'RE **GOBLINS.**
NAINAI LILJA?
ARE YOU AWAKE? I BROUGHT...NEWS.
NEWS? IS THAT WHAT YOU CALL IT?
YOU'VE BROUGHT TROUBLE, ORIEN. INEVITABLE, MUCH-NEEDED, AND *WELCOME* TROUBLE.

IT'S OKAY, ZULI.
TELL HER WHAT YOU TOLD ME ABOUT THE BIRDS.
WE ARE NOT TELLING ANYONE ANYTHING. WE JUST NEED TO --
HA!
I KNEW YOU WERE NO ORDINARY OWL THE MOMENT I SAW YOU.
NOTHING CAN HIDE FROM THESE OLD EYES.
AND DON'T BE AFRAID, LITTLE ONE.
TELL US YOUR TALE.
ALL THE NAINAI ARE LISTENING.

THE SOULS OF DEAD BIRDS HAVE BEEN STOLEN. I LEFT THE GREAT TREE TO FIND OUT WHY, BUT I DON'T KNOW WHERE THEY ARE, OR WHO'S RESPONSIBLE.

NO BIRDS WILL EVER BE BORN AGAIN UNLESS ME AND FROWLY SAVE THEM.

A BAD YEAR, SOME SAY. GOBLINS ARE SICK, THEY SAY. OTHERS BLAME THE WINGS WHO LIVE IN THE HIGH PLACES, AND THINK OF HOW TO GET REVENGE.

BUT THE NAINAIS KNOW DIFFERENT.

WE CAN TASTE THE WIND COMING FROM THE NORTH, AND IT IS PART OF A SPREADING SICKNESS.

AN OLD AND GREEDY HUNGER.

THIS IS WHAT WE KNOW: MAGIC BEGAN THIS. MAGIC WILL END IT.

YOU HAVE TO GO NORTH. THAT'S WHAT I'M CERTAIN OF.

YOU'LL GO WITH HER, OF COURSE.
AND FATE WILL PROVIDE THE REST.
FATE, AFTER ALL, IS WHAT BROUGHT YOU TOGETHER.
NAINAI, YOU WANT ME TO LEAVE? NOW? WHEN I'M BEHIND ON QUOTA?
BESIDES, SHE'S NOT CLAN!
ORIEN...
WILL YOU CHOOSE HIGH, OR WILL YOU CHOOSE LOW?
BUT HE'S RIGHT. GOING NORTH WITHOUT ANY DIRECTION WILL WASTE TIME WE DON'T HAVE.
GOING NORTH WITH THIS ONE WILL WASTE MORE THAN TIME.
CHILD.
YOU HAVE THE MEANS.
YOU HAVE HEART.
YOU HAVE FRIENDS...

WE ARE ALL BORN AT A CROSSROADS, WITH MANY PATHS BEFORE US.
AND ALWAYS THERE IS A CHOICE.
WE CAN CHOOSE TO KNEEL DOWN, OR STAND. WE CAN CHOOSE TO HIDE, OR FIGHT.
I'M AFRAID, NAINAI LILJA. AFRAID OF THIS WORLD, AFRAID OF WHAT I DON'T KNOW...
BUT I'M MORE AFRAID OF NOT HELPING MY FRIENDS.
WE HAVE TO STOP THIS. NO MATTER WHAT.
UM, EXCUSE ME, BUT I HAVE A LIFE HERE. YOU NEED ME. I NEED...I NEED...
I NEED TO NOT GO AWAY. THAT'S MY CHOICE.
THEN YOU'LL FIND WHAT YOU NEED. YOU'LL FIND THE SOURCE.
AND WHATEVER HAPPENS AFTER THAT...WELL...YOU STILL WILL HAVE A CHOICE.
THERE. YOU. ARE.
DRIVER, WAIT!

DIRTY LITTLE HORN-HEAD! COMING HOME AGAIN WITHOUT SCAVENGE? TOO COWARDLY TO SAY SO TO MY FACE?
HOO! HOOO!
AND YOU BRING A STRANGER?
I THINK YOU MUST REALLY HATE LIFE. OR YOU ACTUALLY LIKE BEING STOMPED ON LIKE A PIECE OF NO-GOOD SCRAP.
BY THE STONE GODDESS, LEAVE THEM BE.
WE'RE SURVIVING BY THE TIPS OF OUR WINGS, NAINAI LILJA. EVERYONE IS HUNGRY, AND WE'VE ONLY GOT THREE MONTHS TO PAY FOR WINTER HAVEN.
EVERYONE HAS TO WORK TOGETHER. EVERYONE NEEDS TO CONTRIBUTE. AND IF HE CAN'T, THEN GET OUT. ONE LESS MOUTH TO FEED.
STOP!
YOU DON'T SURVIVE BY HURTING EACH OTHER!
AND WHO ARE YOU, STRANGE CHILD?
YOU SMELL LIKE THE SKIES. YOU SMELL LIKE CLOUDS -- WHAT DO YOU KNOW ABOUT WHAT WE HAVE TO ENDURE?

THE CHILD IS MY GUEST.
THEN SHE CAN PAY WITH THE OWL. WE'LL EAT IT FOR SUPPER TOMORROW.
YOU CAN'T!
I'LL HAVE YOU KNOW, OWLS ARE POISONOUS!
WHAT -- IT CAN SPEAK --
I'LL BREAK ITS WING.
A TALKING OWL WILL BE WORTH SOMETHING TO THE GRIFFINS.
I BROUGHT SCAVENGE! THE KIND THAT WILL BUY US A PLACE ON A MOUNTAIN!

NO!
I TRUSTED YOU!
TAKING HER SCAVENGE FOR YOUR OWN, ARE YOU?
NOW THAT IS ONE WAY TO SURVIVE.
HMMM...IT'S JUST SIRIC JEWELRY. EXCELLENT CONDITION, I'LL GIVE YOU THAT, MAYBE ENOUGH TO CLEAR US FOR WINTER HAVEN, BUT --
IT'S MAGIC. I SAW IT WOUND WRAITHS.
DON'T BE STUPID.
OW!
THAT'S MINE. GIVE IT BACK.
I'LL MAKE YOU A VERY GENEROUS DEAL FOR IT. YOU CAN STAY WITH US THROUGH WINTER, NO NEED TO BRING IN SCAVENGE.
NO.

WE'RE LIVING THROUGH DESPERATE TIMES. I'M AFRAID YOU DON'T HAVE A CHOICE.
I DO HAVE A CHOICE.
AND I SAID NO.
AHH!
FOOLS! DANGER IS COMING!
ZULI, RUN!

THE CHILD IS STILL WITH THE GOBLINS, CAPTAIN FARA.
I CAN TASTE HER.
REMEMBER, SHE MUST BE TAKEN UNHARMED! NOT A SCRATCH ON HER!

?!
HISS-SS-SSS!
WE'RE AXED! IT'S THE KALINAR!
TO THE WAGONS! SHUT YOURSELVES IN AND FIND YOUR WEAPONS! BUT DON'T ENGAGE UNLESS YOU HAVE NO CHOICE!
LET GO OF ME, ORIEN!
COME ON! KALA WILL LET US HIDE IN HER WAGON!

NO HIDING FOR YOU!
WE NAINAI ARE DECIDED. YOU MUST HELP HER!
BUT WHAT ABOUT --
GO AND DON'T COME BACK!
THIS IS NO LIFE FOR YOU!
THIS IS ALL I KNOW, NAINAI LILJA.
THEN GET TO KNOWING BETTER.
AND COME UP WITH A GOOD APOLOGY FOR ZULI! YOU'RE GOING TO NEED IT!

NNGH!
WHY ARE YOU DOING THIS?
BECAUSE I MUST.
BE GONE!
HISSSSS

FWUP!
DON'T FIGHT, CHILD! I'M NOT GOING TO HURT YOU!
THEN LET ME GO!
THAT IS IMPOSSIBLE.
THE WITCH-QUEEN WANTS YOU.
AND SHE'S BEEN WAITING FAR TOO LONG FOR YOUR RETURN TO GIVE UP. SHE'LL TEAR APART THE WORLD FOR YOU.

BUT WHY?
I'M NO ONE.
WRONG.
YOU'RE THE ONE WHO WAS SAVED.
HNNH?

AAHHH!
RWARR!
IT'S...LIKE...THE WRAITH...THOSE STONES...
I GOT YOU, MONSTER! STAY DOWN!

ZULI?
GET AWAY! I DON'T WANT YOUR HELP!
LOOK, I'M SORRY! I WAS DESPERATE! AND YOUR OWL WAS GOING TO BE SHOT!
I ALWAYS LOVE A GOOD ARGUMENT, BUT LET'S TRY TO ESCAPE FIRST.
GAH! RUN!
SO...WEAK...
BARELY...KNOW...MYSELF...
THE HEX WAS TOO STRONG...
GIRL...YOU SAVED US...
...FREED OUR SOULS FROM WITCH-QUEEN'S CONTROL...

WE MUST FLEE...FROM HERE...BEFORE OTHERS REALIZE...WE ARE FREE...
THERE'S NO WE! YOU JUST ATTACKED US!
YOU EXPECT US TO TRUST YOU?!
IT'S OKAY, FROWLY. I THINK... WE'RE SAFE WITH THEM.
WAIT!
UH...PLEASE DON'T PUSH ME OFF?

PANT... PANT...

OOF!
THUD
SLURRRRRP
THE FETTER...
IT'S BROKEN.
AFTER ALL THESE YEARS...TRAPPED...

NEVER AGAIN!

THE OTHERS SHOULD BE ON OUR HEELS. THEY SHOULD NEVER HAVE ALLOWED US TO ESCAPE.
BUT PERHAPS LOSING ME AND JAX HAS MADE THE WITCH-QUEEN CAUTIOUS.

WHO ARE YOU...AND WHO IS THIS WITCH-QUEEN?
WERE THOSE RED STONES CONTROLLING YOU?

MY NAME IS FARA, AND I AM -- WAS -- CAPTAIN OF THE KALINAR GUARD.
THE KALINARIANS WERE CONQUERED BY THE WITCH-QUEEN AND HER ARMY, AND MY SOLDIERS AND I WERE FED TO HER MAGIC.

THOSE GEMS ARE SOUL-FETTERS.
USED TO BIND US IN AN UNHOLY FASHION TO THE WITCH-QUEEN, AND ENSLAVE US TO HER WILL.

I DIDN'T KNOW ANYTHING EXISTED THAT COULD DESTROY THEM.
THE GRIFFINS HAVE WARDS TO PROTECT THEMSELVES AGAINST THAT KIND OF CONTROL, BUT NOTHING TO DESTROY THEM.
SPLIT THAT.
YOU BOTH NEED TO EAT.
THIS WITCH-QUEEN...COULD SHE BE RESPONSIBLE FOR STEALING OTHER SOULS? LIKE THOSE OF THE BIRDS, AND ALL LIVING THINGS?
STEALING SOULS OUT OF THIN AIR, YOU MEAN?
EVEN SHE'S NOT THAT POWERFUL, I HOPE.
THE WITCH-QUEEN CAME FROM THE NORTH MANY YEARS AGO -- ALONE, WITH NOTHING BUT HER MAGIC -- AND NOW CONTROLS MOST OF THE WEST.
SHE'LL TAKE IT ALL IF SHE CAN. SHE'S ALREADY INFILTRATED MOST ABANDONED SIRIC CITIES WITH HER WRAITH SOLDIERS, TO KEEP THEM SAFE FOR HER EVENTUAL ARRIVAL.

YOU SAID SHE WANTS ME BECAUSE I'M THE ONE WHO WAS SAVED.
I DON'T KNOW WHAT IT MEANS. I'M ONLY REPEATING WHAT I HEARD HER SAY.
"THE ONE WHO WAS SAVED HAS FINALLY RETURNED. EVERYTHING DEPENDS ON FINDING HER."
DO YOU KNOW WHAT THAT COULD MEAN, FROWLY? DO YOU REMEMBER ANYTHING?
ER...NO.
THAT LOOKS SIMILAR TO THE GEM THAT WAS CONTROLLING FARA. IT'S JUST A DIFFERENT COLOR, THAT'S ALL.
ARE *YOU* UNDER SOMEONE'S CONTROL?
I AM OFFENDED BY THE SUGGESTION.
IT WOULDN'T BE YOUR FAULT. YOU MIGHT NOT KNOW.
SHE COULD ALSO BE AFTER THIS. IT'S CERTAINLY A THREAT TO HER POWER. I DON'T SUPPOSE YOU'D --
I'M SORRY, BUT YOU CAN'T HAVE IT.
I WOULDN'T --
MY PARENTS LEFT IT WITH ME.

WHERE WERE THEY FROM?
I DON'T KNOW...THEY ABANDONED ME.
OR SAVED YOU FROM SOMETHING, AND LEFT YOU A USEFUL BIRTHRIGHT.
THEY NEVER CAME BACK. AND I STILL HAVEN'T FOUND ANYONE ELSE LIKE ME.
THERE'S NEVER JUST ONE OF ANYTHING, CHILD.
I...I'VE HEARD THAT BEFORE. BUT I DON'T KNOW IF I BELIEVE IT ANYMORE.
IT'S OKAY IF YOU DON'T BELIEVE. WE ALL SOMETIMES FEEL ALONE, EVEN AMONG OUR OWN KIND.
WISE WORDS, FOR A GOBLIN.
DON'T PATRONIZE ME -- AND DON'T CALL ME THAT. YOUR KIND ALWAYS MAKE "GOBLIN" SOUND LIKE IT'S A DIRTY WORD.
MY KIND?
MOUNTAIN KIND. HIGHLANDS KIND. ALL THE KIND WHO DON'T LET GOBLINS INTO THEIR CITIES WITHOUT MAKING US PAY AND PAY.
THE KALINARIANS DID JUST THAT BEFORE THE WITCH-QUEEN TOOK OVER. SHE DOESN'T CHARGE NEARLY AS MUCH FOR WINTER HAVEN.

HOW DARE YOU IMPLY THAT THE WITCH-QUEEN IS SOMEHOW --
I DON'T CARE IF YOU BOTH KEEP FIGHTING, BUT FIRST -- WHICH WAY IS NORTH?
GOOD RIDDANCE.
HEY!

FROWLY?
THE FEATHERLESS ARE NOT WHAT I EXPECTED.
LIFE IS FREQUENTLY DISAPPOINTING. I REMEMBER THAT MUCH.
FROWLY, YOU LIED EARLIER, WHEN I ASKED IF YOU REMEMBERED ANYTHING ELSE.
I DIDN'T FEEL COMFORTABLE SPEAKING IN FRONT OF STRANGERS.
THAT SIRIC CITY WE APPEARED IN...I KNOW IN MY HEART IT WAS A THRIVING, LIVING PLACE...AND NOW IT'S AN ANCIENT RUIN.
I'M CERTAIN A GREAT DEAL OF TIME HAS PASSED IN THIS WORLD SINCE YOU WERE LEFT AT THE TREE.
YOUR FAMILY IS GONE, ZULI. IF I HAD ANY FAMILY, THEY'RE GONE, TOO.
I KNOW.
BUT YOU, CHEERA, LITTLE RED...T'AIA AND THE GUARDIANS...
...WERE THE BEST FAMILY I COULD HAVE EVER HAD.
YOU'RE MY PARENTS.
I LOVE YOU, FROWLY.
OH...OH MY...

FROWLY, LOOK AT ALL THOSE BIRDS. SO MANY DIFFERENT KINDS, MORE THAN I EVER IMAGINED.
IS THAT WHAT YOU CALL A MIGRATION?
IF IT WASN'T ENTIRELY THE WRONG TIME OF YEAR FOR THAT SORT OF THING...
...AND THE WRONG KINDS OF BIRDS TRAVELING TOGETHER.
SOME BIRDS ARE PICKY ABOUT WHO THEY'LL FLY WITH.
FEAR WILL MAKE ANY BIRD ACT AGAINST ITS NATURE.
ZULI! COME BACK THIS INSTANT!
HELLO?
OH!
YOU'VE ALL LEFT YOUR NESTS?

EVERY BIRD WHO CAN FLY, AND EVEN THOSE WHO CANNOT.
WE ARE LEAVING THE NORTH. THE FEAR IS THERE.
WHAT IS THE FEAR?
WE DO NOT KNOW. BUT WE CAN FEEL IT. THE WIND TASTES LIKE A SNARE.
SUNSETS GLITTER LIKE THE EYES OF A CAT.
THE TREES SHIVER AND WHISPER TO EACH OTHER OF A SPREADING SICKNESS IN THE SOIL.

NAINAI LILJA SAID SOMETHING SIMILAR.
THE ANSWERS MUST BE THERE. I JUST HAVE TO FIND THEM.
WE KNOW YOU DO.
YOU ARE THE TWO-LEG HUNTING THE WIND.
YOU KNOW ME?
NO OTHER TWO-LEG, OR FOUR-LEG, CAN TALK TO US.
RED BIRD SAID YOU MIGHT COME. SAID WE ALL HAD TO HELP. MANY DID NOT BELIEVE HIM, BUT NOW...NOW IS DIFFERENT.
THE WIND IS TOO STRONG.
LITTLE RED? YOU'VE SEEN HIM?
NO. LITTLE BIRD TOO LITTLE AND WORLD TOO BIG.
BUT BIRDS TALK. BIRDS SHARE. ESPECIALLY NOW, WHEN THOSE OF US IN NORTH FEEL DANGER.
OUR KIND GO WHERE OTHERS DON'T.
SEARCH. LOOK FOR STRANGE THINGS.
MIGHT HAVE FOUND SOMETHING.
BEYOND LAST MOUNTAIN, ACROSS WATER THAT IS SKY.
CANNOT FLY CLOSE. WIND TOO SICK. BUT HEAR RUMORS OF STRANGE FIRE. BLUE, LIKE ICE.
COULD YOU TAKE US THERE?

CANNOT. MUST LEAD WING-MATES AWAY. YOUNG AND OLD.
ALL MUST LIVE.
I LIKE BEING ALIVE.
BESIDES, YOU HAVE HIM.
EVEN IF HE IS NOT ONE OF US.
PARDON ME? I'M EVERY INCH AN OWL.
NO!
MORE THAN, LESS THAN.
NOT WANT TO BE YOU.
LET'S GO.
HAHA
I THINK WE'VE LEARNED ALL WE CAN FROM THEM.
IF YOU SAY SO, FROWLY.
THANK YOU ALL FOR YOUR HELP!
SAFE FLYING TO ALL OF YOU!

I WONDER WHERE LITTLE RED HAS GONE?
THE WORLD IS BIG. HE COULD BE ANYWHERE.
ARE YOU OKAY, FROWLY?
DON'T BE WORRIED BY WHAT THE OWL AND RAVENS SAID ABOUT YOU.
I'M NOT. NOT AT ALL. NOT EVEN A LITTLE.
I JUST HAVE NO INTEREST IN FLYING TOWARD ANYTHING CALLED FEAR, THAT'S ALL.
NEITHER DO I.
BUT SOMEONE HAS TO.

DON'T WORRY, I WON'T GET IN YOUR WAY.
BUT NAINAI LILJA WANTED ME TO HELP YOU...AND...AND I HAVE NOWHERE ELSE TO GO.
ABOUT BEFORE...I KNOW YOU WERE SCARED. I WAS SCARED, TOO.
AND I KNOW WHAT YOU DID MIGHT HAVE SAVED FROWLY.
THANK YOU FOR THAT.
BUT?

BUT NOTHING.
THANK YOU.
DO YOU MISS YOUR FAMILY? ARE YOU WORRIED THEY'RE OKAY?
THEY'RE MY CLAN, BUT NONE OF THEM ARE BLOOD. I'D BEEN ON MY OWN FOR YEARS, BUT NAINAI LILJA CONVINCED DRIVER TO TAKE ME IN.
I MISS HER. AND KALA. THE REST, TOO, I GUESS.
IT'S HARD BEING A GOBLIN WITH NO CLAN.
NO ONE LIKES US MUCH.
NAINAI LILJA SAYS IT'S OLD HISTORY, SOME WAR BETWEEN US AND THE
THAT NO ONE WON.
THAT WAS ANOTHER LIFE.
T'AIA SAID WE ALL ARE GIVEN MANY LIVES SO WE CAN START ANEW.

COME.
WE NEED TO KEEP MOVING.
YOU MUST WANT TO GO HOME, CAPTAIN FARA.
YOU DON'T...YOU DON'T HAVE TO HELP.
DON'T WE?
YOU FREED US.
JAX IS RIGHT. BUT EVEN IF WE DIDN'T OWE YOU...YOU NEED HELP.
AND HELPING YOU, I SUSPECT, WILL HELP US ALL.
SO IT'S NOT OUT OF THE GOODNESS OF YOUR HEART.
ORIEN.
WHAT'S IT GONNA COST US?
HE'S RIGHT. I AM SELF-SERVING.
I HAPPEN TO BE TOO DESPERATE FOR COMPLETE ALTRUISM.
BUT WE DO HAVE SOME HONOR LEFT...DON'T WE?
I HOPE SO, FARA.
I DON'T WANT TO IMAGINE WE'RE THAT BROKEN.

DEAR TREE...IF YOU CAN HEAR ME...
HELP ME FIND LITTLE RED AND ALL THE SOULS OF THE BIRDS, PLEASE.
HELP ME FIND THE SOULS OF THE GOBLINS, AND ANYONE ELSE WHO HAS BEEN TAKEN.

PLEASE HELP ME FIND THE COURAGE. I'M SCARED.
HELP ME NOT GIVE UP.
DO YOU PRAY TO ROCKS, ORIEN?
I PRAY TO THE STONE GODDESS. SHE LIVES IN THE EARTH, BUT ESPECIALLY STONE. AND MOUNTAINS ARE HOLY BECAUSE THAT'S WHERE SHE IS THE MOST.

WHAT DO YOU KNOW ABOUT THE SIRIC?
NOT MUCH. THEY MADE ART, MAGIC, MUSIC. THAT KIND OF STUFF DOESN'T SURVIVE WELL, ESPECIALLY WHEN EVERYONE WHO MADE IT DISAPPEARS ALL AT ONCE.
WHAT DO YOU MEAN... ALL AT ONCE?
THE SIRIC VANISHED. THAT'S WHAT THE STORIES SAY.
ONE DAY THEY WERE THERE, AND THE NEXT DAY THEY WERE GONE, LIKE THEY NEVER EXISTED. IT WAS A YEAR AFTER THE WAR BETWEEN US AND THEM HAD ENDED.
EVEN THE OTHER WINGS COULDN'T BLAME THEIR DISAPPEARANCE ON US. IT WAS TOO WEIRD.
WHERE DID THEY GO?
DUNNO. BUT THEY LEFT EVERYTHING BEHIND.
A LOT HAS BEEN PICKED OVER BY NOW, BUT I SCAVENGE FOR ANYTHING THAT COULD STILL BE INTERESTING.
ONE TIME I FOUND PARTS OF A NECKLACE. I DON'T KNOW IF IT WAS MAGIC, BUT THAT GOT ME ON DRIVER'S GOOD SIDE FOR A WHILE.
GOBLINS ARE THE ONLY ONES WHO STILL GO INTO SIRIC CITIES. IT'S FORBIDDEN, BUT EVERYONE PRETENDS NOT TO NOTICE BECAUSE THEY LOVE OLD SIRIC STUFF.

AND BECAUSE THEY'RE NOT WILLING TO GO THERE THEMSELVES. SCARED THEY'LL DISAPPEAR, TOO, I THINK.
OWL?
YES, CAPTAIN?
I'VE HEARD STORIES THAT IT WAS COMMON AMONG THE SIRIC TO HAVE BIRDS LIKE YOU AS COMPANIONS.
BIRDS WHO COULD TALK. WHO WERE...MORE THAN WHAT THEY SEEMED.
I ASSURE YOU, I'M VERY ORDINARY.
HARDLY.
I'VE NEVER SEEN THE WITCH-QUEEN'S FACE, BUT SHE HAS COMPANIONS JUST LIKE YOU.
IT MAKES ME WONDER.
AND WHY WOULD I CARE?
BECAUSE I THINK YOU AND ZULI ARE MYSTERIES, EVEN TO YOURSELVES.

"AND THAT COULD BE DANGEROUS."

OH MY.

IS THIS REAL?

OOOF!
GASP

THIS IS WHAT I WAS TAUGHT.
THAT EVERYTHING WAS FIRE AND DESPAIR, AND ENDLESS MADNESS.
I LEARNED THAT THE WORLD DIED. AND WE WOULD HAVE DIED WITH IT.
BUT THE TRUTH IS NEVER WHAT IT SEEMS.
AND NEITHER ARE YOU.

I HAD TO SEE YOU FOR MYSELF.
EVEN IF IT'S ONLY IN DREAMS.
WHO ARE YOU?
SOME CALL ME A WITCH. OTHERS CALL ME A CONQUERER.
BUT I AM NONE OF THE THINGS PEOPLE IMAGINE ME TO BE.
I AM MERELY...A WOMAN WHO LEARNED TO PLAN.
AND I'VE BEEN WAITING FOR YOU, ZULI.
TOGETHER WE CAN MAKE AT LEAST ONE THING RIGHT.
BUT MAYBE ALL OF IT.
THEY SHOULD NEVER HAVE THROWN ANY OF US AWAY. IT WASN'T OUR FAULT. WE WERE BABIES.
AND THEY STILL HAVEN'T LEARNED THEIR LESSON.
WHAT --
"WE'LL MEET AGAIN."
"SOON."
AAAH!

FROWLY? WHERE --
QUIET. WE NEED TO RUN.
THE HUNT HAS FOUND US.

PANT...
PANT...
IT'S NO USE GOING ANY FARTHER. THEY'LL CATCH UP BEFORE LONG.
ORIEN, YOU CAN GLIDE, YES?
KEEP GOING! STAY IN THE AIR AS LONG AS POSSIBLE!
JAX AND I WILL TRY TO LURE THEM AWAY!

WAIT, THERE'S SO MANY! AND JAX IS EXHAUSTED.
I'M A FYREFOX. ALL I NEED IS A MOMENT. DON'T WORRY FOR ME.
I DON'T KNOW ANYTHING ABOUT BIRD SOULS, BUT WE CAN'T LET YOU OR THAT BRACELET FALL INTO THE WITCH-QUEEN'S HANDS.
TAKE CARE OF EACH OTHER.

COME ON! WE CAN'T WASTE THIS CHANCE SHE'S GIVEN US!
UH, ZULI...I'VE NEVER BEEN THIS HIGH UP BEFORE.
I THINK I'M SCARED OF HEIGHTS.
BUT YOU'VE FLOWN BEFORE!
NOT REALLY!
I ALMOST NEVER HAVE A CHANCE TO GLIDE!
YOU'VE ALREADY SEEN I'M TERRIBLE AT IT!

LITTLE TWO-LEG!
TELL HIM TO NOT FIGHT SO HARD!
THE AIR WILL HOLD YOU! HAVE FAITH!

THE EAGLE WAS RIGHT!
THANK YOU!
WING TO WING, LITTLE TWO-LEG! WE ARE WATCHING FOR YOU!
NNN.
IT'S SO BEAUTIFUL UP HERE!
MORE BEAUTIFUL THAN I COULD HAVE IMAGINED!
TELL ME WHEN IT'S OVER.

...PANT...PANT...
SO. TIRED.
HA HA HA!
HA HA!

WITH ALL THIS SPACE, WHY CAN'T YOUR PEOPLE LIVE IN MOUNTAINS? ESPECIALLY IF THEY'RE HOLY TO YOU?!

IT'S TO PUNISH US...BECAUSE OF THAT WAR I MENTIONED.

WE'RE GLIDERS, YOU SEE.

WE CAN ONLY REALLY FLY FROM HIGH PLACES, WHICH MEANS THE LOWLANDS MAKE OUR WINGS USELESS UNLESS IT'S STORMING OUT AND THE WINDS ARE STRONG.

WE'VE JUST HAD TO ADAPT TO LIFE ON THE GROUND, THAT'S ALL.

SOMETIMES...WE EVEN FORGET WE'VE GOT WINGS. THAT'S THE JOKE, ANYWAY.

THOUGH WHEN I WAS LITTLE...I'D CLIMB TO THE TOPS OF TREES AND THROW MYSELF OFF. OVER AND OVER.

I'D FLY AS FAR AS I COULD.

UNTIL ONE DAY I JUST...STOPPED.

I WISH FARA AND JAX WERE HERE.
I HOPE THEY'RE OKAY.
YEAH? THE KALINAR ARE GOOD AT TAKING CARE OF THEMSELVES.
THAT'S RATHER CALLOUS.
YOU'D SAY THE SAME ABOUT GOBLINS, I'M SURE. YOU DON'T LIKE US MUCH.
WELL...
GASP!
IS THAT...ME?
YOU'VE NEVER SEEN YOURSELF?
NO.
RUSTLE

WELL, PERHAPS BREAKFAST WOULD STEADY MY NERVES...
OH!
I ALWAYS WONDERED WHERE OTI CAME FROM!
I STOLE HER FROM A TRADER LAST WINTER.
WAIT!

MEEP!
MEEP!
MEEP!
WAIT!
OTI!
THAT'S...NOT...NICE!

BEHIND YOU!
WHUMP!
COME ON!
NNGGH!
THWAP!

LET...HER...GO!
WHAT IS THAT THING?! ONE OF THE WITCH-QUEEN'S SOLDIERS?
IT'S A MOUNTAIN SPIDER! AND THIS IS JUST HOW THEY ARE!
BUT IT'S WEARING A COLLAR!

PANT...
PANT...
THAT WAS THE SECOND MOST FRIGHTENING EXPERIENCE OF MY LIFE.
HMMM...
IT'S OKAY, LITTLE ONE. YOU'RE SAFE.
PLEASE EXPLAIN TO ME WHY YOU'RE FOLLOWING THE MASSIVE SPIDER THAT JUST TRIED TO KILL US?!
I CAN'T LET THOSE OTHER... FURRY WINGS...STAY CAPTURED.
WE HAVE TO DO OUR BEST TO RESCUE THEM.
IF WE CAN'T EVEN DO THAT, HOW CAN WE BE EXPECTED TO SAVE THE SOULS OF THE BIRDS?
I WOULD ARGUE IT WOULD BE EASIER TO SAVE THE SOULS OF THE BIRDS IF WE'RE NOT SPIDER FOOD.
I HATE TO SAY IT, BUT HE'S RIGHT.
AND THOSE COLLARS?
WHY DO THEY RESEMBLE MY BRACELET?

THIS IS ABSOLUTELY... ABSOLUTELY...NOT OKAY.
I DIDN'T KNOW THERE WAS A SIRIC CITY IN THESE MOUNTAINS. IT'S NOT LISTED ON ANY MAP.
THE SCAVENGE MUST BE --

WELL, WHAT HAVE MY DARLINGS BROUGHT ME NOW?

LITTLE HEARTS POUNDING? THE WARM SCENTS OF FUR AND SUNLIGHT AND FOREST?

ALL TOGETHER, YOU BARELY SEEM LARGE ENOUGH FOR A SINGLE BITE.
AH...BUT OUR OTHER GUEST... SHE MIGHT MAKE A MORE SUCCULENT MOUTHFUL...
...THOUGH IT HAS BEEN ENDLESS YEARS SINCE I SCENTED HER KIND.

YOU KNOW WHAT I AM?
YOU'VE MET MY PEOPLE BEFORE?
COME CLOSER, SO I CAN BE CERTAIN.
NO, THANK YOU.
FLY, FLY, FLY.
I THINK YOU'RE QUITE CERTAIN ALREADY.
BRAVE LITTLE THING.
BUT YOU ARE IN MY HOME, AND MANNERS MUST BE OBSERVED.
WHEN A DRAGON MAKES A REQUEST, ONE MUST ALWAYS OBEY.
YOU AREN'T AFRAID, ARE YOU?
I AM, BUT I'M CURIOUS, TOO. I'VE NEVER MET A DRAGON BEFORE.
I HADN'T EVEN HEARD OF THEM UNTIL RECENTLY.
FOR THE RECORD, *I'M* VERY AFRAID.

NEVER HEARD OF A DRAGON?
I'D BE AMUSED, THOUGH PRUDENCE DEMANDS I TAKE CARE.
A DAY COULD COME WHEN WE ARE RARE ENOUGH THAT SUCH A STATEMENT MIGHT NOT BE SO...CHARMING.
YOU DIDN'T ANSWER MY QUESTION.
WHY, YOU ARE A CHILD OF THOSE WHO MADE THIS CITY, AND ALL CITIES LIKE IT.
I WOULD KNOW A SIRIC IN MY SLEEP, THOUGH IT HAS BEEN ALMOST A THOUSAND YEARS SINCE YOUR PEOPLE FLED THESE LANDS.
AND YOUR KIND, WITH THEM.
BUT WHERE ARE YOUR WINGS, CHILD?
I'VE NEVER HAD WINGS.
I ONLY HAVE THIS.
I'M TOLD IT'S MAGIC AND THE SIRIC MADE IT. BUT IT LOOKS THE SAME AS THE COLLARS YOUR SPIDERS WEAR.
BECAUSE IT IS ***DRAGON-MADE.*** THE SIRIC ALWAYS CAME TO ***US*** WHEN THEY NEEDED MAGIC-SMITHS, WHICH WAS OFTEN.

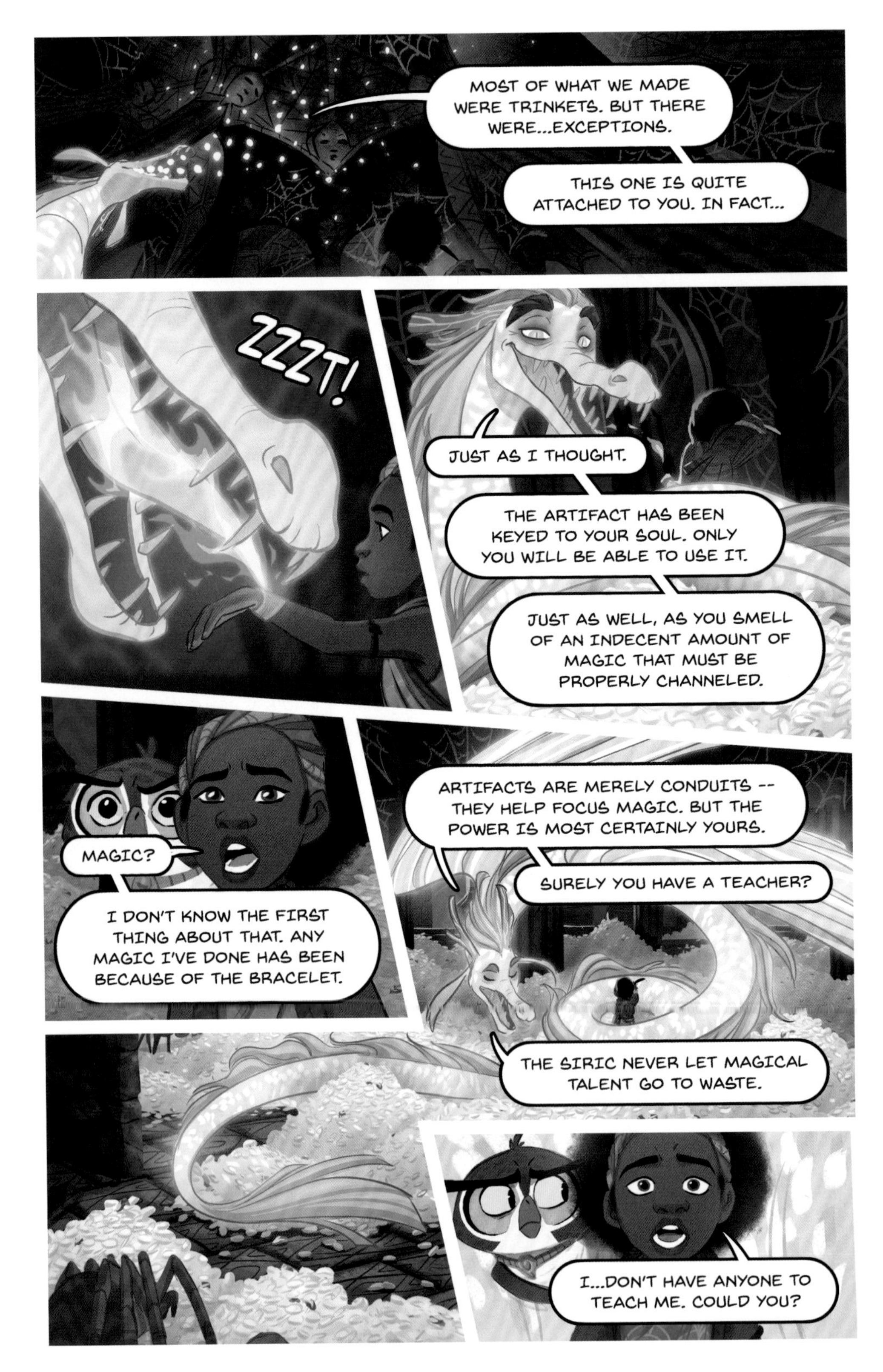
MOST OF WHAT WE MADE WERE TRINKETS. BUT THERE WERE...EXCEPTIONS.
THIS ONE IS QUITE ATTACHED TO YOU. IN FACT...
ZZZT!
JUST AS I THOUGHT.
THE ARTIFACT HAS BEEN KEYED TO YOUR SOUL. ONLY YOU WILL BE ABLE TO USE IT.
JUST AS WELL, AS YOU SMELL OF AN INDECENT AMOUNT OF MAGIC THAT MUST BE PROPERLY CHANNELED.
MAGIC?
I DON'T KNOW THE FIRST THING ABOUT THAT. ANY MAGIC I'VE DONE HAS BEEN BECAUSE OF THE BRACELET.
ARTIFACTS ARE MERELY CONDUITS -- THEY HELP FOCUS MAGIC. BUT THE POWER IS MOST CERTAINLY YOURS.
SURELY YOU HAVE A TEACHER?
THE SIRIC NEVER LET MAGICAL TALENT GO TO WASTE.
I...DON'T HAVE ANYONE TO TEACH ME. COULD YOU?

THAT'LL HAVE TO WAIT.
I THINK NOT. I WOULD RATHER EAT YOU. IN FACT, I MIGHT HAVE DONE THAT ONCE ALREADY TO ANOTHER APPRENTICE.
IF YOU EXIST, THE SIRIC MUST STILL BE OUT THERE, SOMEWHERE. FIND ONE OF THEM.
I'M BEING HUNTED BY SOMEONE CALLED THE WITCH-QUEEN, BUT I CAN'T LET HER CAPTURE ME. I'VE GOT A JOB TO DO. THE SOULS OF DEAD BIRDS ARE DEPENDING ON ME.
THEY'RE NOT COMING HOME TO THE GREAT TREE. THE SAME MIGHT BE TRUE FOR THE SOULS OF OTHER LIVING CREATURES.
I'M TRAVELING NORTH TO SEE IF I CAN FIND WHO'S TAKEN THEM.
WHAT DOES A MITE LIKE YOU KNOW ABOUT THE GREAT TREE?
ABOUT ANY OF THE GREAT HAVENS?
IN FACT SHE KNOWS NOTHING. PLEASE, ZULI, TIME TO LEAVE.
I WAS RAISED THERE BY THE SPIRITS WHO GUARD THE SOULS. I'M A HELPER, TOO. JUST LIKE THEM.

NOT LIKE THEM, CHILD. NOT EVEN I COULD PRESUME TO EQUAL MYSELF WITH THE GUARDIANS OF THE HAVEN THAT TAKES THE SOULS OF DRAGONS.
BUT PERHAPS I WILL NOT EAT YOU, AFTER ALL.
A LIVING CHILD RAISED IN A GREAT HAVEN? HOW ODD YOUR TREE ALLOWED ITS GUARDIANS TO DO SUCH A THING.
WHAT IS IT LIKE? THE HAVEN OF THE BIRDS?
A VERY SAFE PLACE. SO SAFE.
IT IS...A TREE THAT GROWS FROM THE HEART OF THE EARTH INTO THE STARS. EVERY LEAF HUMS.
WHAT IS YOURS LIKE?
I CANNOT SAY, CHILD. THE LIVING HAVE NO MEMORIES OF THE SLEEP AFTER DEATH. THERE ARE STORIES, OF COURSE. OF A VAST MOUNTAIN CAVERN WHERE WE ARE BORN AGAIN IN FIRE.
UNLIKE BIRDS, DRAGONS LIVE A LONG TIME, AND WE PRODUCE FEW CLUTCHES OF YOUNG. I DARESAY WE PERISH MORE THAN WE ARE REBORN.
THAT IS VERY SAD.
I HAVE OFTEN THOUGHT SO. BUT WE ARE NOT ALWAYS FRIENDLY TO OUR OWN KIND, SO PERHAPS IT IS FOR THE BEST. THE WORLD MIGHT NOT SURVIVE IF THERE WERE TOO MANY DRAGONS UPON IT.
OR PERHAPS THE WORLD WOULD SEEK TO DESTROY US FIRST.
GREED, AFTER ALL, IS THE BEGETTER OF MISERY.
I WAS JUST LOOKING! I'LL PUT THEM BACK!

ORIEN.
WE'VE GOT NO CLAN. WE'LL NEED COIN, ZULI.
AND I DIDN'T THINK ANYONE WOULD NOTICE. THERE'S SO MUCH.
IN THE WRONG HANDS, EVEN A TINY THING CAN CAUSE IMMENSE PAIN.
FOR YOUR ATTEMPTED THEFT, I SHALL SIMPLY HAVE TO EAT YOU, YOUNG GOBLIN.
WHICH IS A SHAME, GIVEN HOW CLOSELY YOUR KIND ONCE WORKED WITH DRAGONS.
YOU CAN'T! HE'S...HE'S MY FRIEND. AND I NEED FRIENDS, SIR DRAGON.
IT'S OKAY TO MAKE MISTAKES, ISN'T IT? ESPECIALLY IF YOU LEARN FROM THEM?
NO.
ZULI, IT'S OKAY. DON'T...DON'T TAKE UP FOR ME. I'M NOT WORTH GETTING HURT OVER.
YOU'RE WRONG, ORIEN. THE DRAGON IS WRONG, TOO.
AND HE KNOWS IT.

THIS IS WHY I DON'T SPEND TIME WITH YOUNG PEOPLE ANYMORE.
IN EXCHANGE FOR MY BENEVOLENCE, HOWEVER, THE GOBLIN BOY WILL OWE A DEBT.
PAYABLE TO ALL DRAGONS WHO REQUIRE AID...NO MATTER HOW DIRE OR IMPOSSIBLE THE TASK.
THEY WILL KNOW HIM BY THE RING...
...WHICH WILL BE PART OF HIM UNTIL HE DIES.
THIS IS...SO COOL!
PLEASING YOU WAS NOT MY INTENTION!
I WON'T LET YOU DOWN, I PROMISE! I'LL BE THE BEST DRAGON APPRENTICE EVER!
ER...

WE SHOULD GO.
EVERY MOMENT MEANS ANOTHER BIRD LOST TO THE WORLD.
THE RAVENS TOLD ME THERE'S A PLACE NORTH OF THE LAST MOUNTAIN, ACROSS WATER THAT LOOKS LIKE SKY. IT'S A PLACE WHERE BLUE FIRE CAN BE FOUND.
I NEED TO GO THERE. DO YOU KNOW WHERE IT MIGHT BE?
BEYOND THESE MOUNTAINS IS THE SEA. AND THE ISLAND BEYOND THE SEA IS PART OF A VOLCANO THAT HAS GONE SO COLD EVEN DRAGONS DO NOT CALL IT HOME.
THE SEA, THE ISLAND, ARE ALL PART OF THE ABYSSAL CHAIN. VERY FEW REMEMBER THAT PART OF THE WORLD, EVEN THOUGH IT WAS ONCE THRIVING AND GREEN.
BUT THERE'S ONLY ONE THING BLUE FIRE COULD BE, AND THAT IS MAGIC.
A MITE LIKE YOU SHOULD NOT GO THERE. IF YOU EVEN CAN.
I HAVE TO TRY. THE BIRDS TELL ME A BAD WIND IS COMING FROM THAT PLACE. SICKNESS IS SPREADING, AND THAT SICKNESS MEANS SOULS AREN'T COMING HOME WHEN THEIR BODIES DIE.
IT COULD BE YOUR SOUL, MY SOUL, ALL SOULS. THERE'S NO WAY TO KNOW, IS THERE? NOT UNTIL IT'S TOO LATE.

LESS THAN A DAY'S FLIGHT FROM HERE, BY GOBLIN WINGS, IS A SMALL CLOISTER. GLIDE TOWARD THE TWIN PEAKS. FOLLOW THE RIVER BENEATH YOU. WATCH FOR THE WATERFALLS.

A GRIFFIN LIVES THERE. HER NAME IS HIERAN.

THANK YOU SO MUCH.
WHY DO YOU STAY HERE? AREN'T YOU LONELY?
I AM OLD, CHILD. AND MOSTLY BLIND.
THIS IS NO LONGER A WORLD WHERE A DRAGON IN MY CONDITION MIGHT SURVIVE BEYOND THE SAFETY OF A MOUNTAIN KEEP.
AND WHILE I DO NOT FEAR DEATH, I AM RELUCTANT TO LOSE MEMORIES OF THIS LIFE IN MY REBIRTH.
I HAVE LOVED. I HAVE BATTLED. I HAVE BUILT AND DESTROYED. I HAVE TRAVELED FAR. I HAVE FELT JOY AND I HAVE FELT SORROW.
THAT IS PRECIOUS TO ME. I WOULD REST HERE ANOTHER CENTURY IN SAFE SOLITUDE TO HOLD ON TO THOSE MEMORIES.
DO YOU UNDERSTAND WHAT DEATH IS, CHILD? DEATH IS LOSING ALL THAT MADE US. DEATH DOES NOT DESTROY OUR SOULS...BUT IT DOES ERASE THEM.

I DON'T BELIEVE THAT. I BELIEVE EVERY LIFE REMAINS PART OF US. WHY, THE GUARDIANS OF THE GREAT TREE LISTEN TO THE STORIES OF EVERY SOUL WHO RESTS IN ITS BRANCHES.
THOSE SOULS REMEMBER THEIR LIVES, EVEN AFTER DEATH. THEY REMEMBER EVERYTHING.
AND I BELIEVE THAT I DO NOT, IN THIS MOMENT, REMEMBER THE LIFE I LIVED BEFORE THIS ONE.
AND THAT GRIEVES ME.
THE GUARDIANS SAY THAT WE FORGET SO THAT WE MIGHT LIVE. THAT WE CAN'T BEGIN FRESH IN A NEW LIFE BURDENED BY THE PAST. EVEN IF THAT PAST IS WONDERFUL.
WE'D ALWAYS BE THINKING OF EVERYTHING BUT THE PRESENT AND THE FUTURE.
WE'D BE THINKING OF WHO WE WERE, INSTEAD OF WHO WE CAN BE.

YOU ARE OFFENSIVELY OPTIMISTIC. I SHOULD EAT YOU FOR THAT, ON PRINCIPLE.
PLEASE DON'T EAT ME. I'M SO VERY GLOOMY AND PESSIMISTIC.
BUT YOU HAVE EARNED MY CURIOSITY. AND...MY RESPECT.
YOU ARE FREE TO STAY A WHILE LONGER...
...EVEN THOUGH I KNOW YOU WILL NOT.
YOU'VE BEEN VERY KIND, SIR DRAGON. THANK YOU...FOR NOT EATING US.

I MUST EAT, YOU KNOW.
IF NOT NOW, THEN LATER. A REPRIEVE WILL NOT SAVE ALL OF THEM...NOT FOR LONG.
OH, FINE.
YOU ARE A SILLY, NAÏVE LITTLE THING.
AFTER I'VE SAVED THE SOULS OF THE BIRDS, I'LL COME BACK AND VISIT YOU. I PROMISE.
I...LOOK FORWARD TO THAT.

WAIT.
I HAVE NO MAGIC TO GIVE YOU...NO MORE THAN YOU ALREADY POSSESS...BUT I WISH YOU LUCK, LITTLE ONE.
I WISH YOU ALL LUCK.
THAT IS NO SMALL THING, COMING FROM A DRAGON.
IT'S SO BEAUTIFUL...
...LIKE THE GUARDIANS ARE WITH ME AGAIN.

YES, MY FRIENDS...
SHE IS ANOTHER MEMORY I WISH TO HOLD ON TO.

HOW DO YOU FEEL, FINDING OUT YOU'RE A SIRIC?
YOU HEARD THAT?
MY EARS DON'T STOP WORKING WHEN I SCAVENGE.
I HEARD A LOT OF THINGS THAT WERE STRANGE, BUT THAT MADE PERFECT SENSE.
IT DOESN'T TO ME. I DON'T HAVE WINGS.
I WONDER WHAT MY WINGS WOULD LOOK LIKE?
I'M SURE...I'M SURE THEY WOULD BE EXTRAORDINARY.

CAN I SEE YOUR BACK?
NO SCARS. THAT'S GOOD.
YOU THOUGHT SOMEONE MIGHT HAVE CUT OFF MY WINGS?
WHEN I WAS A BABY? WHO WOULD DO THAT?
I'VE SEEN IT BEFORE. NOT ON KIDS, BUT ON GROWN-UPS WHO DO BAD THINGS.
HAVING NO WINGS IS THE WORST PUNISHMENT A WINGED THING COULD EVER ENDURE.
ALMOST AS BAD AS HAVING WINGS BUT NOT BEING GIVEN A PLACE TO FLY?

I'VE DECIDED I'M NOT GOING TO LET THAT STOP ME.
I'LL JUST FIND A BUNCH OF DRAGONS AND LIVE WITH THEM. I CAN DO THAT NOW.
THE DRAGON SAID GOBLINS USED TO WORK WITH HIS KIND. MAYBE YOU'RE JUST FOLLOWING TRADITION.
I'D NEVER HEARD THAT BEFORE, NOT EVEN FROM NAINAI LILJA. THEN AGAIN, I DON'T KNOW ANOTHER GOBLIN WHO'S EVER MET A DRAGON.
COME ON, FROWLY!
YES, LET'S HURRY.
THERE'S SOMETHING IN THE WIND THAT UNSETTLES ME. THE SOONER WE'RE OUT OF THE SKY, THE BETTER.
MAYBE THIS GRIFFIN WILL HELP.
WHAT ARE THEY LIKE?
KINDA LIKE YOUR OWL. A LITTLE STUFFY AND ANXIOUS.
EXCUSE ME --

I HOPE THIS GRIFFIN LETS ME STAY WITH YOU.
THEY'RE THE ONES WHO ENFORCE THE RULES ABOUT KEEPING GOBLINS AWAY FROM MOUNTAINS.
SHE'LL HAVE TO. OR ELSE WE'LL LEAVE TOGETHER.
THANK YOU...FOR WHAT YOU SAID TO THE DRAGON. YOU TOOK UP FOR ME. YOU COULD HAVE GOTTEN HURT.
YOU SAVED MY LIFE BEFORE. YOU DIDN'T HAVE TO.
DOES THIS MAKE US FRIENDS?
ISN'T THAT WHAT I CALLED YOU?
YEAH, BUT YOU MIGHT NOT HAVE MEANT IT.
I DON'T KNOW HOW TO LIE.

GASP
CAREFUL! WE NEED THE GIRL ALIVE!

CAN'T YOU FLY FASTER?
I'M A GLIDER, REMEMBER? IT ALL DEPENDS ON THE WIND!
MAGIC, WE NEED HELP.
GASP
NO, NO, NO!
OOF!

WE'VE GOT YOU!
WHO ARE THEY?
HARPIES! MANTICORES!
I'VE NEVER SEEN THEM THIS FAR EAST!
ONLY DISABLE THE GOBLIN WHEN YOU'RE CERTAIN YOU CAN CATCH HER!
I CAN CATCH HER.

AAAH!
ORIEN!
GRRR!
GET BACK!
GODDESS!

THEY'RE ONLY CHILDREN! STRIKE!
NO, NO, NO...
I HAVE TO SAVE THE BIRDS, I HAVE TO SAVE THE BIRDS.
I CAN'T DIE YET, I CAN'T --

ZULI!
WHAT'S HAPPENING? WHY AM I --
I HAVE WINGS!

FINALLY.
LET US GO!
HUSH. THE WITCH-QUEEN DOES NOT WISH TO HURT YOU.
BUT MISBEHAVE AND --
THE EAGLES!
MMPH!

TWO-LEG, WE HEARD YOUR CALL FOR HELP!
AAAHH!
AHHH!

WAKE UP AGAIN, BRACELET!
SCHHP!
WHAT IS WRONG WITH THESE EAGLES?!
YOU FILTHY... OVERGROWN...CAT!
MEEP!

UH, MAYBE WE SHOULDN'T BE CUTTING THESE ROPES...
FROWLY, WAIT --
NOOOO
WELL, THE MYSTERY DEEPENS.

ARGENTUS WAS WISE TO WARN ME YOU WERE COMING.
NOT THAT HE NEEDED TO. YOU SUMMONED ME QUITE WELL ON YOUR OWN...
...WHICH WILL PLEASE *NO* ONE.
A GRIFFIN!

YOU'VE BROUGHT THE WITCH-QUEEN'S MERCENARIES INTO OUR SKIES.
YOU CHILDREN ARE A BAD OMEN, INDEED.
THANK YOU AGAIN!
WING TO WING...WE FLY TOGETHER. WE FIGHT TOGETHER.

"IF YOU HAD TOLD ME THAT THE FIRST SIRIC CHILD TO BE SEEN IN A THOUSAND YEARS WOULD COME TO MY DOOR, AND BE HUNTED BY THE WITCH-QUEEN, I'D HAVE HAD A GOOD CHUCKLE OVER MY TEA."
"BUT THE REST OF YOUR STORY IS EVEN MORE FANTASTICAL... AND DISTURBING."
IT'S ALL TRUE, MISS HIERAN. 
HASN'T ANYONE NOTICED BIRDS AREN'T BEING BORN? NO ONE'S SEEN THEM FLYING AWAY FROM THE NORTH?
WHO NOTICES BIRDS, ZULI? THEY'RE SO SMALL AND THEY HIDE THEIR NESTS SO WELL.

IF A SMALL THING IS IN TROUBLE, IT'S ONLY A MATTER OF TIME BEFORE BIG THINGS ARE, TOO.
ARE GRIFFINS STILL BEING BORN?
YES. OF COURSE.
ZULI, MAY I SEE THE ARTIFACT ON YOUR WRIST?
SIR DRAGON SAID IT WAS DRAGON-MADE.
SIR DRAGON'S NAME IS ARGENTUS, AND HE IS VERY, VERY OLD, AND VERY GRUMPY. HE ALSO USED TO BE A FAMED SMITH, THOUGH HE STOPPED CRAFTING SEVERAL HUNDRED YEARS AGO.
HE TOLD YOU NOTHING ABOUT WHO MADE THIS?
NO. ALL HE SAID WAS IT WOULD HELP ME DO MAGIC...AND THAT I HAVE...A LOT INSIDE ME.
ARGENTUS WAS NOT WRONG ABOUT THAT...
OH...THAT FEELS LIKE...LIKE A RIVER...
OR...OR FLIGHT...

PARDON ME, MAGUS HIERAN.
THE MAESTRA WISHES TO SEE YOU.
NOW.
MAKE YOURSELVES COMFORTABLE. I'LL RETURN LATER THIS EVENING.
BUT THERE'S NO TIME.
I NEED TO TALK TO YOU ABOUT MAGIC...THE KIND OF MAGIC THAT COULD STEAL SOULS. AND I NEED DIRECTIONS TO THE ABYSSAL CHAIN, BEYOND THE MOUNTAINS. ARGENTUS SAID YOU COULD HELP ME.
YOU SHOULD KNOW, TOO, THAT THE WITCH-QUEEN MUST BE ABLE TO FOLLOW ZULI. HER AGENTS ALWAYS SEEM TO KNOW WHERE WE ARE.
IF WE STAY HERE, YOU SHOULD BE READY FOR ANOTHER ATTACK.
WE'RE ALWAYS READY.

WHAT MADE YOU THINK IT WAS A GOOD IDEA TO RESPOND TO A MAGIC SUMMONS, HIERAN?
IT WAS A MOST EXTRAORDINARY CALL FOR HELP.
AND IT WAS NOT JUST I WHO CAME, BUT ALL THE GREAT PREDATORS OF THE SKY. THE CHILD SUMMONED US ALL. I HAVE NEVER FELT NOR SEEN THE LIKE, MAESTRA.
THAT SHOULD HAVE BEEN YOUR FIRST WARNING. IT COULD HAVE BEEN A TRAP. IT MIGHT STILL BE.
WORSE, YOU HAVE DRAGGED US -- AND PERHAPS ALL GRIFFINS -- INTO DIRECT CONFLICT WITH THE WITCH-QUEEN.
WE HAVE HER PERSONAL GUARD LOCKED INSIDE OUR POTATO CELLAR.
SO? DON'T WE BELIEVE THE WITCH-QUEEN IS TO BLAME FOR WHAT'S HAPPENED TO US?
NOT A SINGLE GRIFFIN EGG HAS HATCHED IN MONTHS. HOW CAN WE IGNORE WHAT THE CHILD SAID?
WE'RE NOT IGNORING HER. WE'RE GATHERING MORE INFORMATION.

WE SHOULD STILL ALERT THE INCANTIC COUNCIL. IF NOTHING ELSE, THEY'LL WANT TO KNOW A SIRIC CHILD HAS BEEN FOUND...
...AND THEY'LL WANT TO KNOW ABOUT THE ARTIFACT THAT'S BONDED TO HER, AND THAT SHE IS ACCOMPANIED BY ONE OF THE LEGENDARIES.
I DARED NOT EVEN LOOK AT HIM.
THE IMPLICATIONS OF THAT ALONE --
SHE HAS NO WINGS, HIERAN. IT'S IMPOSSIBLE THAT SHE'S A SIRIC.
BESIDES, NOT ONE OF THEM HAS BEEN SEEN IN A THOUSAND YEARS, BUT SUDDENLY A CHILD OF THEIR RACE APPEARS...
...CLAIMING TO BE FROM SOME MYSTICAL TREE WHERE BIRD SOULS GO TO BE REBORN?
BIRDS DON'T EVEN HAVE SOULS. IT'S RIDICULOUS.
MAESTRA...SOME OF WHAT THE CHILD SAID MIGHT SEEM FARFETCHED...
...BUT WHAT SHE TOLD ME ABOUT THE NORTH MIGHT BE THE ANSWER WE'VE BEEN SEARCHING FOR.
IT COULD ALSO BE A RUSE FROM THE WITCH-QUEEN.
BESIDES...ARGENTUS IS MY MENTOR, AND A FRIEND. HE WANTS ME TO HELP THE CHILDREN. I CAN'T SIMPLY --
NO.
ZULI HAS THE BLESSING OF ARGENTUS. HE EVEN BLESSED THE GOBLIN BOY, AND BONDED HIM TO A DRAGON-SMITHED ARTIFACT.
THAT'S AN EXTRAORDINARY HONOR, MAESTRA.

WHO ARE YOU LOYAL TO, HIERAN? GRIFFINS OR DRAGONS? GRIFFINS OR CHILDREN WHO ARE NOT OUR OWN?

IT WOULD CAUSE A PANIC AMONG OUR KIND IF THE TRUTH WAS KNOWN THAT NONE OF OUR EGGS ARE HATCHING.

NO, WE MUST QUESTION BOTH CHILDREN FURTHER. THE GOBLIN FIRST, AS WE'LL WANT TO TRANSPORT HIM OFF THE MOUNTAIN AS SOON AS POSSIBLE.

HAVE THEM SEPARATED. AND TELL COOK TO SWEETEN THEIR NEXT MEAL WITH MOONBERRY JUICE.

WHEN THEY FALL ASLEEP, WE'LL BE ABLE TO TAKE ZULI'S ARTIFACT AND STUDY IT.

I WISH I COULD SUMMON THOSE WINGS AGAIN.
I FLEW, ORIEN. JUST FOR A MOMENT.
AND IT WAS...WONDERFUL...
MAYBE YOU COULD USE YOUR MAGIC TO LEVITATE WITHOUT WINGS? YOU COULD CARRY US BOTH...
...OUT OF HERE.

ZULI, HURRY...WE HAVE NO TIME...
GASP
LET'S GO. PLEASE.
IT'S JUST STONE. IT CAN'T HURT US.
ZULI! STOP --

OH NO.
WHAT DOES THIS MEAN?
THAT THING EATING WINGS IS SUPPOSED TO BE A GOBLIN.
THAT'S HOW ARTISTS USED TO DEPICT THE WAR BETWEEN US AND THE SIRIC.
FROWLY WAS RIGHT...LET'S GO.
IT LOOKS SO AWFUL. NO WONDER WE'RE NOT ALLOWED ON THE MOUNTAINS.
I FEAR THE REASONS ARE MORE COMPLEX THAN THAT...

...AND DEEPLY UNFAIR.
CAPTAIN FARA! YOU'RE ALIVE!
HOW...HOW DID YOU FIND US?
I'M A TRACKER. AND SOMETIMES THE ANIMALS OF THE FOREST WILL TALK WITH ME.
AT A CERTAIN POINT IT SEEMED LIKELY YOU MIGHT MEET THE GRIFFINS WHO LIVE IN THESE MOUNTAINS.
MAGIC ATTRACTS MAGIC.
AND THIS IS WHERE YOUNG GRIFFIN MAGES ARE SENT TO LEARN THEIR CRAFT. IT KEEPS EVERYONE ELSE OUT OF HARM'S WAY.
I WASN'T PREPARED, THOUGH, FOR YOU TO JUST LAND IN MY LAP.
SOMETHING ABOUT YOU SEEMS DIFFERENT, CAPTAIN FARA.
ARE YOU...WELL?
NO.

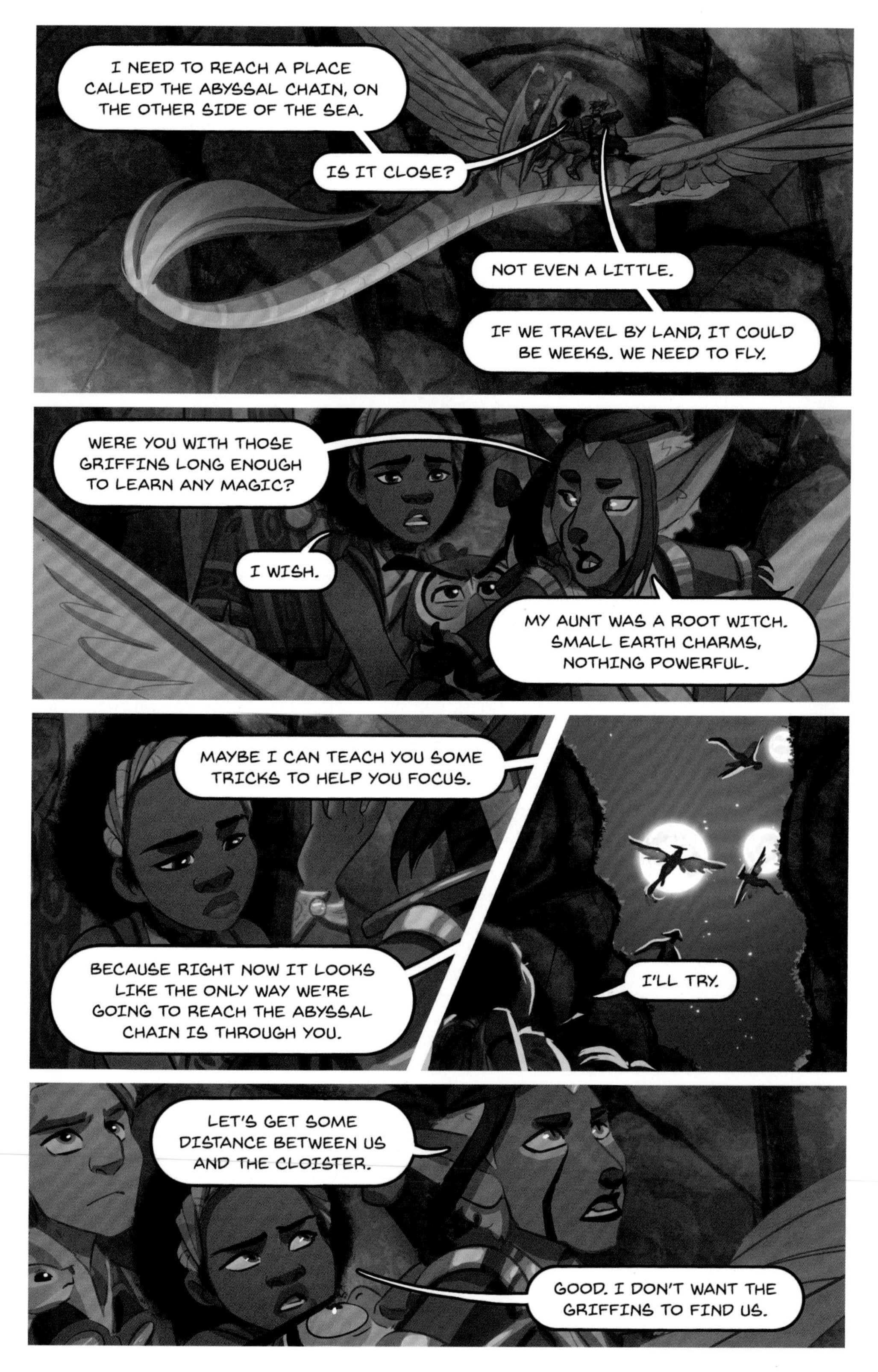
I NEED TO REACH A PLACE CALLED THE ABYSSAL CHAIN, ON THE OTHER SIDE OF THE SEA.
IS IT CLOSE?
NOT EVEN A LITTLE.
IF WE TRAVEL BY LAND, IT COULD BE WEEKS. WE NEED TO FLY.
WERE YOU WITH THOSE GRIFFINS LONG ENOUGH TO LEARN ANY MAGIC?
I WISH.
MY AUNT WAS A ROOT WITCH. SMALL EARTH CHARMS, NOTHING POWERFUL.
MAYBE I CAN TEACH YOU SOME TRICKS TO HELP YOU FOCUS.
BECAUSE RIGHT NOW IT LOOKS LIKE THE ONLY WAY WE'RE GOING TO REACH THE ABYSSAL CHAIN IS THROUGH YOU.
I'LL TRY.
LET'S GET SOME DISTANCE BETWEEN US AND THE CLOISTER.
GOOD. I DON'T WANT THE GRIFFINS TO FIND US.

MEDITATION IS SOMETHING WE'RE TAUGHT AS SOLDIERS.
HOW TO STILL THE MIND IN THE MIDST OF CHAOS.
IT'S PERHAPS THE HARDEST LESSON TO LEARN.
BUT YOU START WITH BREATHING.
AND THINKING ABOUT SOMETHING THAT YOU LOVE.
WHAT DO YOU LOVE, ZULI?
DON'T ANSWER ME. JUST FEEL IT.
LET THAT LOVE MOVE THROUGH YOU...UNTIL NOTHING ELSE EXISTS.
LET IT SINK THROUGH YOU INTO THE AIR YOU BREATHE, THE GROUND YOU SIT ON...LET THAT LOVE BECOME PART OF EVERYTHING AROUND YOU...
AND WHEN YOU ARE GROUNDED IN THAT FEELING, ANCHORED IN IT...
...ENVISION WHAT YOU MOST DESIRE. HOLD IT. TASTE IT. TURN IT AROUND INSIDE YOUR MIND.

"OPEN YOUR EYES, ZULI."

ZULI...
BIRD SOULS! I THOUGHT YOU'D DISAPPEARED!
...WE REMEMBER YOU WITH US...
...LIFE AFTER LIFE...
...AGAIN AND AGAIN...
WHY ARE YOU HERE AND NOT IN THE TREE?
JUST DIED...
...TRIED TO FLY TO TREE...BUT PULLED AWAY...
...STILL BEING PULLED...
...BUT YOU CAUGHT US...
CAN YOU TELL ME WHO IS PULLING YOU?
NO...NO...
...BUT IT IS COLD...
...AND HUNGRY...
...WE ARE SCARED
...DON'T LET GO...
...DON'T LET GO...
NO!

ORIEN!

ARE YOU HURT?
I COULD FEEL THEM, ORIEN...THOSE SOULS...THEY WERE SO AFRAID...
AND WHEN THEY WERE PULLED FROM ME, I SENSED SOMETHING ON THE OTHER END, JUST FOR A MOMENT...
...AND IT WANTED TO EAT ME, TOO.

YOU HAVE SO MUCH POWER, ZULI...
...ENOUGH TO WREST THE SOULS OF THE BIRDS AWAY FROM THEIR CAPTORS, EVEN IF JUST FOR A MOMENT.
YOU BARELY USED THE RELIC.
YOU HELPED ME SUMMON THE BIRD SOULS.
I JUST HELPED YOU FOCUS ON WHAT YOU WANT MOST.
WHAT I WANT MOST IS TO SAVE THEM.
I WANT THAT, TOO, ZULI.
I WANT TO SAVE US ALL.
ZULI...COME AWAY FROM CAPTAIN FARA.

NNGH!
GASP
FARA!
HARPY!
I'M GOING TO TEAR YOU APART!
W-WHAT DO WE DO?
D-DON'T PULL OUT THE BOLT. N-NOT YET. TH-THAT'S ALL I KN-KNOW.
ZULI...HELP ME...

HOW?!
TELL ME AND I'LL DO IT!
USE...YOUR MAGIC...
...BREATHE...
...AND IMAGINE YOUR MAGIC IS A RIVER...RUNNING INTO ME...THROUGH THE BRACELET...
ZULI...I DON'T KNOW IF THIS IS WISE...

I FEEL THE RIVER...
...AND THE RIVER...
...IS INSIDE...
...YOU...TOO...
FINALLY.
ZULI, STOP!

AHHH!
FARA!
WHAT HAVE YOU DONE TO HER?
NOTHING! I WAS TRYING TO HEAL --

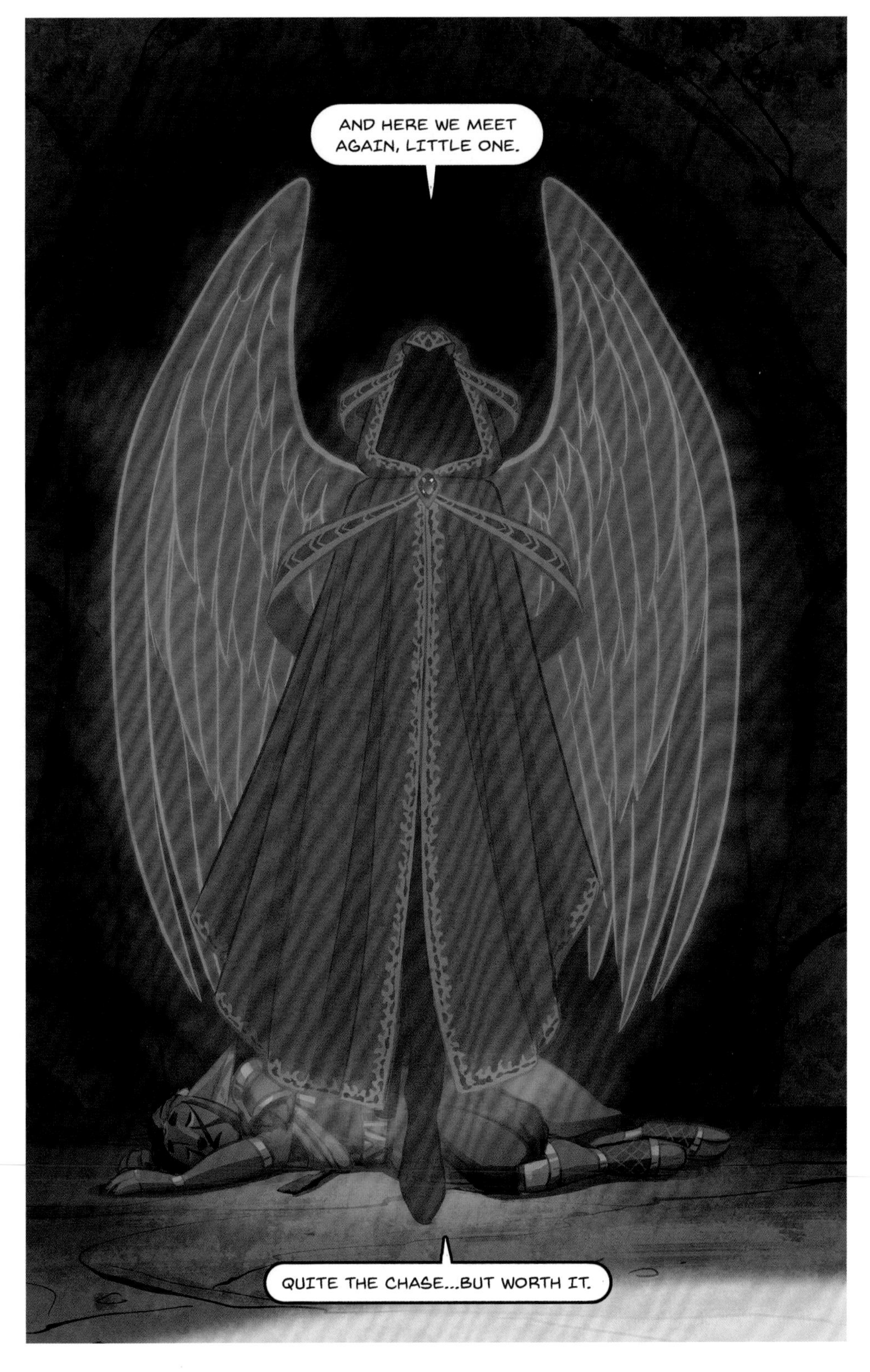
AND HERE WE MEET AGAIN, LITTLE ONE.
QUITE THE CHASE...BUT WORTH IT.

YOU'RE THE WITCH-QUEEN.
HAVE YOU BEEN INSIDE FARA ALL THIS TIME?
ALAS, NO.
THE HUNT CAUGHT THE CAPTAIN, AND RATHER THAN RETURN HER TO MY FOLD, I DECIDED IT WOULD BE BETTER TO WATCH YOU THROUGH HER EYES...
SHE WAS EXQUISITELY VULNERABLE TO REPOSSESSION, HAVING BEEN MINE ONCE BEFORE.
NO, NO, NO...
YOU'RE A GHOST.
I'M A PROJECTION.
WITH AN ARMY AT MY BACK, I WOULD HAVE COME HERE IN PERSON.

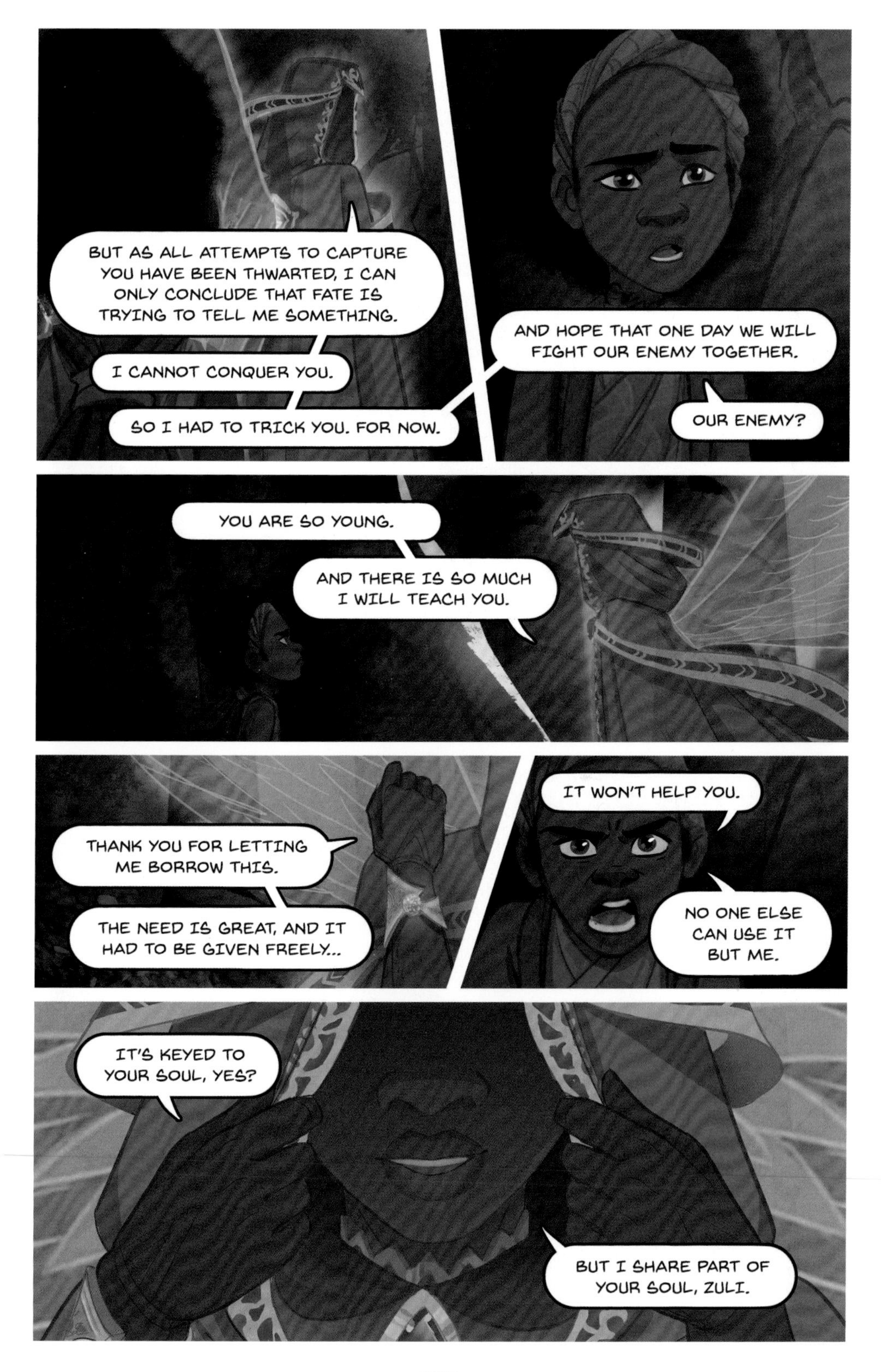
BUT AS ALL ATTEMPTS TO CAPTURE YOU HAVE BEEN THWARTED, I CAN ONLY CONCLUDE THAT FATE IS TRYING TO TELL ME SOMETHING.
I CANNOT CONQUER YOU.
SO I HAD TO TRICK YOU. FOR NOW.
AND HOPE THAT ONE DAY WE WILL FIGHT OUR ENEMY TOGETHER.
OUR ENEMY?
YOU ARE SO YOUNG.
AND THERE IS SO MUCH I WILL TEACH YOU.
THANK YOU FOR LETTING ME BORROW THIS.
THE NEED IS GREAT, AND IT HAD TO BE GIVEN FREELY...
IT WON'T HELP YOU.
NO ONE ELSE CAN USE IT BUT ME.
IT'S KEYED TO YOUR SOUL, YES?
BUT I SHARE PART OF YOUR SOUL, ZULI.

I AM YOUR TWIN SISTER.

SENT TO ANOTHER HAVEN BY OUR PARENTS, TO BE RAISED BY THE DEAD.

I LEFT MY HAVEN EARLIER THAN YOU, THAT'S ALL. AND I'M SURE YOU'VE REALIZED BY NOW THAT TIME MOVES DIFFERENTLY IN THAT PLACE.

WHAT...
THE CAPTAIN STILL HAS A CHANCE, IF YOU HURRY.
I TOLD MY HARPY TO WOUND, NOT KILL.
FIND ME. WE'LL SAVE THE SOULS TOGETHER.
AND I'LL TELL YOU ABOUT OUR PARENTS.
ZULI.
ZULI!

JAX! FROWLY!
GO TO THE GRIFFINS! WE NEED THEIR HELP!
I DIDN'T KNOW.
HOW DID I NOT KNOW THERE WAS ANOTHER CHILD?
HOLD IT TOGETHER, OWL. WE BOTH GOT A SHOCK.
IT'S OKAY TO CRY. I WON'T TELL ANYONE.

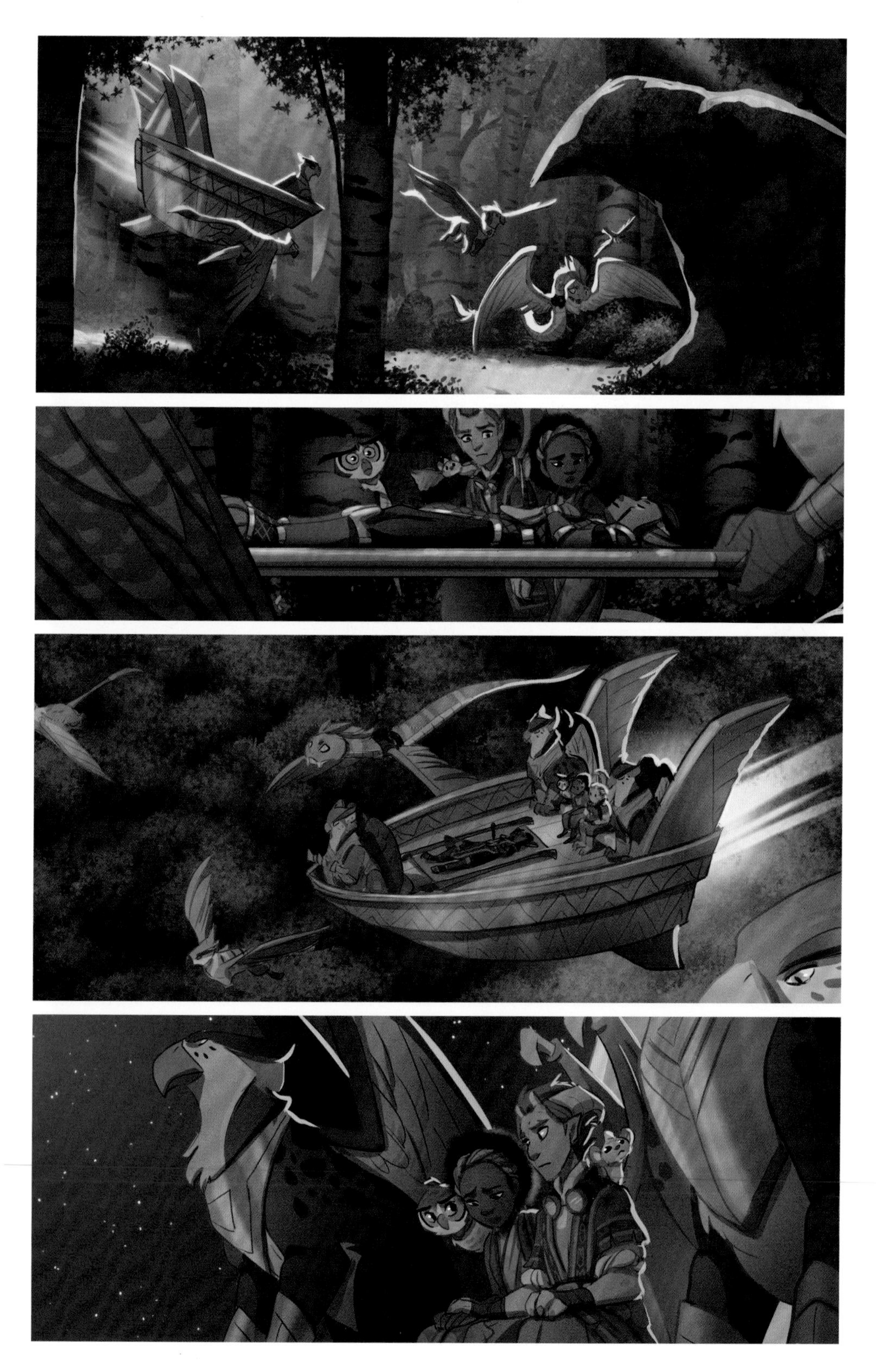

THE WITCH-QUEEN'S
FORCES ATTACKED NOT
LONG AFTER YOU LEFT.

MOST ESCAPED, BUT SOME OF OUR NOVICES WERE TAKEN CAPTIVE.
I'M SORRY FOR WHAT HAPPENED...
...BUT WHAT ARE YOU GOING TO DO WITH US?
YOU AND ALL YOUR FRIENDS ARE BEING TAKEN TO THE CAPITAL FOR INTERROGATION.
WE ARE NOW AT WAR, AND YOU ARE VALUABLE TO OUR ENEMY. THAT MAKES YOU VALUABLE TO US.
YOU WERE SUPPOSED TO HELP US. THAT'S WHAT THE DRAGON PROMISED.
BELIEVE ME...I HAVEN'T FORGOTTEN.

DEAR TREE...
I'LL FIND A WAY TO SAVE THE SOULS...

...BUT WHY...
...WHY DIDN'T YOU TELL ME I WASN'T ALONE?

ACKNOWLEDGMENTS

MARJORIE: First, for my cousin Maya. Many years ago, we would run into the woods surrounding our grandmother's house and search for fairies. We'd adventure for hours, climbing trees, living in other worlds. Now she's all grown-up, but those other worlds still exist—and I think we both still visit them. So, thank you, Maya—for being you, for all the wonderful days of being family together. Love you always.

And for my goddaughter India, as well—who asked for a book about a girl just like herself: brave and kind, who never gives up. I hope you see yourself in Zuli—and no, I haven't forgotten about the blue-haired pirate queen!

Finally, my deep gratitude and appreciation for Teny, who joined me on this journey into a new world, and brought it to life with tremendous vision and love.

TENY: The deepest of heartfelt thanks to the incomparable team at HarperCollins Publishers, whose incredible work, uplifting enthusiasm, collaborative spirit, saintly patience, and human compassion made the completion of this book a possibility. Andrew Eliopulos, Alexandra Cooper, Allison Weintraub, Erin Fitzsimmons, and David Curtis, you are nothing short of saints. An equally huge thank-you to Marjorie Liu, an absolute gem, for trusting me to bring her beautiful story to life and allowing me this opportunity to fall in love with this world. Thank you for your contagious enthusiasm, passion, kindness, compassion, collaboration, and beautiful spirit.

A million thanks to my beloved family. To my darling parents, Hilda and Nejdeh, thank you for your encouragement, optimism, and unshakable love and support. Thanks, Shawnt, bro, for your support and for asking me if I was finished every few weeks (ha!). Matt, my love, thank you for believing in me and reminding me that I could do it. Lana and Shogher, thank you for your emotional support through the darkest of days.

A monumental thank-you to my dearest friends—my Tenydo Studios crew—who have supported me in every way humanly possible throughout this challenging project. Your love and emotional support, especially through the hardest of days, kept my soul together and my spirit alive. Thank you for the daily video chat company, spontaneous food deliveries, jajangmyeon reserve, face masks, muscle creams, etc. You are the definition of true, unwavering friendship, my dazzling, award-winning, multidisciplinary Tenydo Studios: Susey Chang, Estella Tse, Grace Kum, Celine Kim, Jennifer Shang, Kellye Perdue, Kat Park, and Sylvia Lee.

And a shout-out to my entire awesome Armenian family, who are probably going to buy a copy of this graphic novel in support! Hello, Gretta morkoor, Sato, Silva, Lillian, Varand, Vahik, and everyone else! I love you all! Getseh Hye joghovoort!